The Cowboy's Baby Surprise

THE COWBOY'S BABY SURPRISE

The Halligans of Montana

KAZ DELANEY

The Cowboy's Baby Surprise
Copyright© 2024 Kaz Delaney
Tule Publishing First Printing, September 2024

The Tule Publishing, Inc.

ALL RIGHTS RESERVED

First Publication by Tule Publishing 2024

Cover design by Lee Hyatt Designs

No part of this book may be used or reproduced in any manner whatsoever without written permission except in the case of brief quotations embodied in critical articles and reviews.

This is a work of fiction. Names, characters, places, and incidents are products of the author's imagination or are used fictitiously. Any resemblance to actual events, locales, organizations, or persons, living or dead, is entirely coincidental.

AI was not used to create any part of this book and no part of this book may be used for generative training.

ISBN: 978-1-962707-76-3

Dear Reader,

I admit it, the secret baby trope is one that will grab me every time, even one with a slight twist such as this one. Though, if I'm honest, everything about babies grabs me. It took until our children were well and truly grown for me to stop getting all blubbery (*and for my husband to finally sigh with relief*) over teeny knitted bootees and bonnets at fairs and fetes. So, setting out to find gorgeous baby Mia's daddy—or at least writing about it—was something that gave me great joy, and I'll also admit to many tears.

However, cute as she was, baby Mia wasn't all that held me in this story. You know, for authors, it's a heady feeling to be able to make dreams come true; kind of powerful and yet humbling. Both JD Halligan and Evie Davis were two people just begging to have their paths cross and their dreams fulfilled—even if they had their heads in the proverbial sand. What's more, when fate brought them together in the shape of a baby girl, it was evident to anyone but themselves that they were perfect for each other.

So, what would any self-respecting romance author do in that situation? Force them into close proximity, of course! What's more, with neither knowing much about caring for a baby, (*well, apart from Evie's self-enforced thirteen and a half hour YouTube tutorial*) they need to join forces and learn together, allowing them to also learn about each other—learn to trust, and that sometimes, you really do need to take a chance because who knows? You might even find your forever person.

I so hope you find yourself cheering for JD and Evie as I did—*and maybe too get gooey over baby Mia, have a few grins and shed a few tears*—cheering on as JD and Evie finally see what has been in front of them all the time. I'm pretty sure Mia knew all along…

Thank you for hanging out with me.

Loads of hugs and lots of book-love,
Kaz xxx

Dedication

For my fabulous editor and friend Kelly Hunter.
For your wisdom, patience, love, friendship and unwavering support.

And

For my beautiful friend Paula J Beavan, for all the zooms, all the chats, all the hand-holding and for reading this ms a million times.

Chapter One

"*Evelyn?* Miss Davis? We seem to have lost you. Warwick was asking about the status of the D'Alessio account. Do you have an update?"

"Update?" *Of course they wanted an update.* Five stern faces stared out through her computer screen—waiting. Watching her flap and flounder; watching her attempt to slow her breathing, to steady her shaking hands, to control the heat rushing to her face. Saw her fail—on all counts.

Where was that folder?

Was it bad to pray for a sudden power outage? A minor earthquake? A cup of coffee accidentally spilled across the keyboard? *Tempting.*

As it was, Evie had barely made it to the Zoom meeting on time, and yes, she'd noted the polite, yet surprised, looks she'd received when she'd first connected. Evie had been ready for it. Told herself she could pull it off, but it was true that strawberry-shaped and styled woolen beanies probably didn't quite go with the somber black business suit jacket and discreetly stylish white shirt she wore under it. What they didn't realize was that the unwashed, unbrushed hair the beanie concealed was way worse. Way worse.

Or that the strawberry hat—a joke gift from her assistant—was in the top three of respectable garments she wore, which said a lot about everything on her lower half, and thankfully hidden from view.

Silence broken only by the shuffle of the odd page loomed loud in her ears; silence that was sounding even more silent as she fumbled through the accumulated paraphernalia littering the table she was working from. *How can one small person be the cause of all this?*

Relief swept in on a wave when she spied the orange folder buried beneath a pile of baby cloths and bibs; relief that was snatched away as quickly as it had arrived when, in her haste, she knocked an open jar of apple sauce onto the hardwood floor.

It wasn't a big noise by noise standards, but in the awkward silence preceding it, it echoed around the room and she stilled. Held her breath. Prayed.

All in vain.

Closing her eyes, she again focused on breathing when the sudden piteous cry of a baby completely filled any blanks in the air around her. Head bowed, she dared not look up at those faces watching; dared not search each one for signs of judgment; or worse, satisfaction they'd proved she wasn't up to this task.

Instead, she made her way to the squirming bundle and clutched it to her chest in a desperate attempt to restore calm.

Theodore Bannister, senior partner of Bannister, Bannister and Trot, lawyers to the rich and powerful, cleared his throat, a not-so-subtle hint that she was still delaying the meeting. *Surely, they had something else to do? To chat about? The weather? Cool for this time of the year in San Fran. Or so she'd heard. She hadn't actually seen the outside world for three days!*

"Miss Davis?"

"Yes, I... um..."

The cries increased in volume. This child had magnificent projection, perhaps she'd become an opera singer—she'd already perfected C-sharp.

Nonetheless, calm definitely wasn't being restored—for either of them—not by jiggling, or patting, or sitting, or threat-veiled suggestions, or whispered begging. Pulling in a deep breath—and keeping the baby out of sight—Evie leaned left, angling her head sideways which was exactly how she appeared on the screen. Sideways. The green woolen stem that sat atop the strawberry hat, drooped toward the desk. One ear flap dangled low, the other landing to cover her right eye. She brushed it aside, allowing her a clear view of five immaculately groomed heads all suddenly angling sideways as well, each one frowning. Oh dear...

She missed the exact wording of Mr. Bannister's muttered curse as he straightened his head, but she guessed some of it was self-directed. She knew, however, that in one of his rare gestures of sharing, the rest was all for her. *Not good.*

Following Bannister's lead, the other members of the meeting also readjusted their positions, straightening, blinking—looking slightly dazed as once more their heads were where they should be.

Contrarily, her boss was suddenly looking very decisive. "Ahem… Evelyn …*Evie*, we understand you have found yourself in an unusual, and undoubtedly difficult, situation but there is also no doubt that this is affecting your work. We suggest you take some time to sort this mess and then resume your duties. Take the next two days. That will run you to the weekend. Hopefully four days will be long enough? Have you located the child's father yet?"

Her neck ached and she wanted to straighten, but for some reason, this position had somehow managed to settle the baby, so she held her ridiculous sideways pose. "Yes, I have. He's apparently a rancher in Montana. I haven't yet made direct contact bu—"

Bannister held up a manicured hand. "Yes, well… Good. We'll expect you on Monday. And by then we also expect you'll have made some progress on the D'Alessio account. I hope I don't need to remind you of its importance."

"No, no… Of course. And yes, four days should do it. Should give me time … *to get there and back*." The last five words had been muttered into the ether; to herself. This time it hadn't been a hand that halted her words, it had been the blank screen. She'd been excused.

It was what she'd wanted, yet, perversely, it burned—and

she tried to rationalize the contradiction by blaming exhaustion. She hadn't slept for a month. Okay maybe it had only been three days but it felt like a month. Three days since she'd been summoned out of the blue to attend a hospital bed. Three days since she'd laid eyes on a friend she hadn't seen since she was ten years old.

Now, thinking about the baby in her arms she conceded that whole situation still felt totally surreal. But what choice had she had? The lawyer in her chimed in to recite a whole litany of them, but none of them stood up against the fear in Hope Reynold's eyes.

On a sigh Evie adjusted her load, the change in weight and movement signaling Mia had fallen asleep again.

Now? You sleep now? Not ten minutes ago?

The sofa called and Evie responded, shuffled toward the decadent cloud of the finest, pure white, kid leather. She'd imagined the care instruction leaflet probably had a sketch of a child on it with a big cross through it. A warning that combining the two would only end in tears.

Lowering herself heavily onto a corner of the sectional, she propped her feet up on the extension, wondering as she did so if she'd ever bothered to do this before the last four days. The sofa was two years old and barely used, forcing her to concede she'd possibly slept on the sofa in her office more often than she had in this apartment. Not quite the luxurious apartment of her dreams, but one she'd filled with beautiful things, at least.

She'd get there. Hard work was the price of success. She knew that, and she was determined to meet that goal. And at only thirty-one, it was paying off. Well, it had been, until three days ago.

As she gently moved Mia, to cradle her properly, the disastrous meeting suddenly replayed in her mind, and her heart kicked up a gear; again her face warmed with... Frustration? Embarrassment? Anger? All of which she felt entitled to. Never, ever, in the ten years of her employ had she *not* been fastidiously prepared. Never, ever, had she let down the team or the firm. She was 100 percent dedicated; they knew that.

And yet, surely... No. She refused to feel sorry for herself. The firm—Mr. Bannister—was being fair. They'd given her leave to take care of this business. And she'd already made progress with that. She'd made all the necessary calls, ordered everything to ensure the father would have all he needed.

All she had left to do, was arrange a flight to Bozeman, and in a few days, all would be back to normal. She'd be back to being the rising star of Bannister, Bannister and Trot. Back to her own life.

Mia's rosebud mouth curled into a smile—*angels whispering sweet nothings?*—and she snuggled in closer, one fat little fist landing on Evie's chest, right at the discreet, lace-trimmed cutout. Against Evie's skin. So incredibly soft, so sweet... Before her brain had registered the intention, she'd lifted that warm little fist, felt it curl around her finger and hold firm; brought it to her lips.

What was she doing? But even as she pulled her lips away, she somehow couldn't make herself unwind those tiny fingers from her own. She stared down at that dimpled fist, noting its perfection. Noting all of little Mia's perfection. Strawberry-blonde wisps of hair played against alabaster skin that would enhance her beauty as she grew older. Exactly like her mother. Hope's hair was reddish gold, so pretty. Just as she had been all those years ago.

Images from that long-ago childhood rushed back at her, of her friend Hope, of the two of them in fifth grade, such tight friends. Of Hope's cute face, and the scattering of freckles across that little upturned nose. Would Mia eventually develop those little freckles?

Their parting back then had been heartbreaking. Evie's mother had managed one of her clean dry spells and regained custody, so Evie was pulled from that foster home and mother and daughter reunited. Of course, it hadn't lasted, and Evie remembered her wretchedness when just a few months later she was placed with yet another family, and no Hope.

She shuddered as other memories tried to fight their way forward. People spoke of something leaving a metaphorical bitter taste, but in Evie's case it was a real thing. There it was now, burning her throat, and did every time she thought of the woman who had given birth to her. Reluctantly untangling her fingers, she reached for the bottle of water sitting on the hand-crafted, crystal-flaked side table, another for the *do not mix with children* list, intent on drowning out those childhood memories. To push them right down deep, into that internal vault she could mostly keep locked.

Distraction had always been her best defense against the memories, and so she deliberately focused on her current problem. Fulfilling her old friend's request and delivering Mia to her father in Montana.

Replacing the water bottle on that elegant table suddenly sent her thoughts swirling down a side avenue. Funny how a mere side table could be that catalyst. Yet, there was nothing mere about that piece of furniture, so was it a catalyst or a metaphor? A metaphor for the life she'd chosen? Had she chosen these things simply for their aesthetic beauty, a tangible example of how far she'd come—or because they were another excuse, or reason, not to have children of her own?

Idly she stroked Mia's whisper-soft curls shutting that thought down before answers could slip forth, forcing her head back to her present dilemma. One finger dipped down to ever so lightly stroke that perfectly rounded cheek, thinking instead about *this* baby's future.

The call from the hospital had been a huge shock, even more so when she'd heard Hope's name. Apparently, Hope had seen Evie's name mentioned in a news report, so knew where to contact her. Of course, Evie hadn't hesitated to go to her, fully prepared to help her childhood friend in any way she could.

However, none of the ways she expected to help out had included the cute bundle in Hope's arms. A baby? A child…

Shock number two, the one that still burned an acid trail each time she thought of it, was that Evie hadn't been the only one called. Child Protective Services had been there waiting.

The image of Hope's face, that day, was one that had stayed with her every waking moment, and plenty of those during her snatched sleep. Every time, especially, she looked at this baby. Hope had begged her to take Mia, to ensure she had a home, that she was loved. That she wasn't subjected to what they'd had to endure as kids—placed with mostly overworked, or uncaring, guardians.

That Evie find Mia's father.

Hope claimed he was a good man, that it wasn't his fault she was alone; that he'd care for his daughter.

And if he didn't? If he refused to accept responsibility? Or worse, if she got a bad vibe?

Evie refused to think that way. Had to trust Hope's instincts. *And right there was obstacle number one.* Who was adult Hope? Evie had no idea—basing her decisions on a child she'd spent less than one year with more than twenty years ago. Sure, they'd been like sisters, but they'd been ten years old! Who was Hope now? Had she grown into a woman whose instincts could be relied upon? And if that answer was negative, where did that leave Evie? Or more specifically, where did that leave Mia? Evie's heart clutched.

She'd vowed from a very young age that she'd never have children, not because she didn't like them, but because she understood what it was like to be a vulnerable child desperately seeking the love and security of someone who truly cared. Children, she'd decided, were precious commodities and should only be with those who could devote their lives to them. And she wasn't prepared to take that risk.

No, finding Mia's father was the best course in the short term. Maybe even long term. Hope was very unwell; her treatment would be lengthy—and even then...

Swallowing back an annoying lump that had landed in her throat, she tucked the baby in a little tighter before reaching for the letter and paperwork Hope had given her—along with detailed instructions about Mia's routine.

The movement stirred Mia, and Evie watched, worried when her own heart melted as the tiny person stretched, and blinked open those incredible brown eyes. Eyes the color of rich dark chocolate, so startling, even with that unusual marking.

Surprisingly happy now, Mia gurgled and wriggled on Evie's lap. At least the little toweling onesie now allowed easier movement. There'd been many lessons learned these past three days. Not the least of which had been that unlike the smart zippered dresses in Evie's wardrobe, Mia's zippered suit didn't fasten down the back. Which also meant the simple little collar wasn't, in fact, a fashionable cowl neckline but a cute little hood. *Who knew?* Not Evie. She suspected Mia may have known though. Especially when the back-to-front outfit left her looking like she was in a straitjacket!

Evie sighed. This enforced crash course on caring for a baby was still a work in progress. Hence the lack of sleep. Teething meant everything in reach would be chewed, including Evie's one-of-a-kind paper sculpture—a Christmas gift from the firm. It would no longer be increasing in value, but she also couldn't question Mia's taste. It had been ugly, making her wonder if Mia would one day be an art critic?

Teething wasn't the only reason for sleepless state. Evie's own nerves hadn't helped. What if something happened to the baby while she slept? What if she threw up? Or choked? Fell out of her crib? Scratched by the cat? These things happened! The fact that Evie didn't even own a cat didn't play into easing her fears. She'd read about this. It was a thing! And she was taking no chances.

Even so, in spite of her exhaustion, she'd found it impossible not to respond to that little face; to that determined little expression, to those big innocent eyes staring up at her.

Like now.

On that first day Evie had accidentally unleashed Mia's giggle when she'd absently pulled a funny face while trying to perfect diaper changing. The baby's response was a giggle that should be bottled and sold as an instant pick-me-up. In these past few days Evie had experimented with many other facial contortions and every one elicited the same wonderful response. Pushing all her other concerns aside for a moment, Evie lost herself in those giggles once more, and as before, completely unable to control her own instant smile in response.

When Mia ended the game in favor of chewing the ear of a soft plastic bear, Evie reached again for Hope's paperwork. She'd read the letter several times. It outlined her brief relationship with a guy from the rodeo circuit, only realizing she was pregnant after he'd left. One thing that stood out was Hope's contention that she'd tried to do everything right throughout Mia's gestation, that she was determined Mia would have the best possible chance.

Given that the first thing Evie did was call in a favor and had Mia checked by a leading pediatrician, that fact appeared to be true. The doctor had declared that not only was Mia perfectly healthy, even if very slightly underweight, but otherwise even advanced for her age.

The weight thing had sat heavy on Evie's shoulders. Mia certainly didn't *look* underweight. But, then again, like herself, Hope was slight, so perhaps Mia would follow suit? It wasn't as if she was scrawny. Her little arms and legs were actually quite chubby—her little fists adorably dimpled.

She shuffled the letter to the back and glanced once more at both the birth certificate and the report from the private investigation agency she'd employed to find the father. It hadn't been difficult. It wasn't like he was hiding. He also didn't seem to have a police record or any other issues that might raise a red flag. Single also, apparently—which should make things less awkward, at least. Parents alive and residing close by. All good things.

Scooping up the baby, Evie kissed her nose. "We're going to find your daddy, little one, and I know he'll just fall in love the moment he sees you. Yep, JD Halligan of Marietta, Montana won't know what hit him."

And surely that little hitch Evie felt in her chest was only indigestion from the left-over baby cereal that ended up being her dinner last night. Had to be it. She hadn't always had a great relationship with carbs, so there was the proof.

HAVING PARKED HIS truck in one of the attached garages, JD Halligan made his way to the sprawling family farmhouse he'd called home for all his thirty-four years. After mopping the sweat off his face with his shirt sleeve, he pushed his hat higher up his forehead and tilted his head to check out the sky. The weather had held for the past couple of days, letting them mend most of that fence damage, and he was crossing everything that it held for a few more days so they could finish up and get the herd down from the high country.

A lightning-fast spear of worry lodged in his chest, instantly halting his progress when he thought he sensed a bit of moisture in the late September afternoon breeze. Frowning, he searched the sky again, seeing nothing but a brilliant expanse of blue—not a cloud in sight. Maybe it would be okay. And maybe he was also astutely ignoring the fact that Montana weather could turn on the flip of a fifty-cent piece.

He was already late getting the herd down and a change now would be costly. It was impossible to think about this extra stress without thinking about the reason, and his fists clenched. While the action threatened to cut off circulation to his hands, it didn't stem the white-hot heat that roared through him like a brushfire.

Sure, the lost time would be costly but not near as costly as losing his prize bulls and the seed that ensured his herds were considered some of the most highly valued in the state. And that's what would have happened if he hadn't stumbled across the plan to steal them by four seasonal ranch hands, all of whom turned out to be nothing more than low-down rustlers.

Blame sat heavily on his shoulders. The whole area had been hit with a run of big storms, and he'd been distracted, working around the clock to plug boundary holes; expecting others were doing their share, trusted where he shouldn't have trusted.

He was damned lucky it had ultimately been a good outcome, but also now meant he was four men down at a time when he not only needed every man on deck, but he also expected they'd all—himself included—be putting in long hours.

They had. He and his remaining crew—and his concern that they were as tired as him was the reason he called a stop to this day much earlier. They all needed sleep, and once he'd washed off all this sweat and dirt, and got something in his belly, that's where he was headed. To bed.

Weariness slowed his long-legged stride and for a moment he thought it was also responsible for the swirl of dust billowing along the lengthy tree-lined drive to the house. A mirage? It took a moment for him to realize it was a truck traveling fast. A big delivery truck—not a farm vehicle—and curiosity propelled his final steps to the house, arriving at the base of the front stairs leading to the porch at the same time as the truck pulled to a stop.

The driver jumped down. Young, animated. "Sorry man! I couldn't find the place. Never been to this part of Montana before. But don't worry, all your gear is here now, all safe and accounted for. Not too late, right?" For the first time since he'd begun to speak there was doubt in his voice.

"Kinda depends on what you've got there. Are you certain this is the right place? I'm pretty sure we weren't expecting a delivery."

The guy glanced at his clipboard. "JD Halligan? Lazy H Ranch?"

JD nodded.

There was amusement in the guy's dark eyes as he rounded to the back of the truck and rolled up the metal door. "You didn't know you were getting this? Ha! Must be a surprise. Helluva way to find out, though." His laughter continued as he boosted himself up on the tailgate lift and climbed into the back. "Wait till I tell the guys this one!"

More intrigued than surprised, JD followed the guy's lead and wandered to the back door, just in time to be handed a large carton bearing an image of something that looked like... Nah, couldn't be. "A baby's high chair?"

Laughing guy was still smirking.

JD's head whirled as a whole array of baby paraphernalia got emptied out of the truck to land at his feet; his wild thoughts frantically trying to find sense. Was this Joanna's? Was his sister pregnant? After a bad breakup Joey was off licking her wounds. Was she in trouble? And had not called him?

Another idea struck, not as worrying, but just as unpalatable. *Was this some ridiculous practical joke?* His brother, Jack, had been ribbing him about finding someone and settling down. All because some of the anxious mothers in Marietta were beginning to circle, earmarking him as good son-in-law material.

The more he thought about it, the more sense this latter explanation made. This had Jack written all over it. Maybe even Leo as well. Just because he hadn't heard from his youngest brother for way too long didn't mean Jack hadn't been in touch with him.

Another carton, this one the approximate size of New Jersey, landed in his arms. Diapers. *Diapers?*

A wide flat box was next. Laughing guy slid it toward him. "The crib, hopefully with instructions. And hey!

Congratulations!"

JD worked his jaw muscle, feeling the tension as his whole lower face tightened. "For the record, I am *not* about to become a father."

"I wouldn't be too sure about that."

JD's head spun to the left. What, this guy was a ventriloquist? But that voice—soft, most definitely feminine, controlled, every word clearly enunciated. His search to find the source continued, turning him a complete one-eighty until he came face-to-face with its owner. And stalled there.

"Pardon me?" He hadn't even heard a vehicle.

The sight was almost too much for his weary brain to contend with. Was this part of the joke? If his brothers had chosen someone they thought he would probably—definitely—get turned on by, they'd done well. If they thought he might think of her as marriage material, they'd got it so wrong.

His past experience flashed through his head on a wave of bitterness. Not for the woman before him, but for what she had fleetingly represented. Like the other woman, the one here in front of him would last about three minutes on a ranch like this.

She was eyeing him carefully, studying him with eyes so blue he could clearly identify the shade even from this six- or seven-feet distance. She, whose perfume closed that distance, something soft and sultry, reaching out to wind itself around him.

She, with the golden hair and golden skin, standing before him in slim pale pink pants, and matching blazer that kind of outlined her figure. And those heels… The jacket was fastened with only one button down low and there was some kind of lacy thing underneath.

Wavy tendrils of hair had slipped from their top knot, and even *almost* more remarkable than the sleeping baby she held in her arms was the weariness etched into that gorgeous face.

Her eyes never wavered and he wondered what was turning over in her mind. Until she spoke. "JD Halligan?"

What was this? *National identification day*? He nodded. It was a measured, reluctant nod, as though identifying himself was going to end up being a very bad decision.

He watched her swallow deeply. "There's um, no way to say this other than simply blurt it out. I've ah, come to deliver your daughter."

The frown on his face carried through his tone. "What? Say again? *Deliver* my daughter? Like a stork or something?" This had gone too far.

"Pardon?" Her obvious confusion prompted an echo of his own frown of moments before. "*A stork?* What are you? Three years old?"

"Which is about the appropriate age for this joke." He raised both hands. "This has gone far enough. I'm done, okay?"

"Ohhh, this is good…"

The woman and JD both turned to laughing guy who was now sitting on the edge of the truck's tailgate, legs swinging, grinning from ear to ear. JD was the first to respond, but only by a second and there was a weird, momentary, sense of connection when they'd both told the guy to butt out. A connection that died the moment JD looked back at her. She was showing no signs of moving.

His gaze narrowed, his sigh long and weary. "Look, I don't know where you came from, but honestly, lady, you look beat and I know I'm beat. So, you can go collect from my brother, or both, tell them the joke backfired—or was a raging success—whatever works best for you, and we can both go get some rest." Turning to laughing guy, he said, "And you can do the same. Pack up this gear and move on. Show time is over."

Laughing guy responded first. "No can do, man. From here I gotta head up north and pick up another load to take back to Bozeman." With a grin and raised eyebrows, he nodded across to the baby. "Looks just like her daddy, I reckon."

Frustration roared through him with the force of a freight train but golden lady's words arrived first. "Mr. Halligan, I assure you this is no prank." Her foot was tapping against the paving stones, the one's he'd laid with his father. It somehow, ridiculously made the joke more inappropriate. "So, I'm sorry, but I can't leave right now. Trust me, though, I'm counting the minutes."

Patience was something he usually had in truckloads. Right now, he'd barely fill a kids' sand pail. "What, you gotta pick up a load up north as well? Twins?"

Laughing Guy laughed. Again. "Hey! That's good!"

This was getting old. "This is not my baby! And I'd appreciate it if you both left my property."

Golden lady shrugged. "I've got a piece of paper here that says otherwise."

"I doubt that very much." He blew out a long, tired sigh. "Okay, so maybe this isn't a joke. Maybe it's a scam. Is that what's going on here? Because I can tell you that unless you had a very long gestation—like two years—that baby is not mine."

Laughing Guy clucked his tongue. "Two years? Man, that's rough. You know, maybe I could fix you up…"

Enough was enough! All he wanted was a shower, a cold beer, a steak, and bed. And nothing else. Except maybe to reclaim his dignity. Turning on laughing guy, he roared, "Get outta here! Now!"

And of course, he woke the baby.

Of course he did.

❦

ROOTED TO THE spot, Evie tried to make sense of that scene as she watched JD Halligan stride up into the house. Did the man not have any manners? Decency? Had he not realized she was coming? But the messages she'd left…

And why was he so sure he wasn't Mia's father? Something wasn't making sense, but despite her exhaustion, she hadn't come this far to be stonewalled.

Her eyes were still glued to that front door, the one he'd passed through, hoping—expecting—he might return. He didn't and for the first time, while soothing Mia, Evie turned to take in the surroundings. The house personified the all-American dream. White siding, solid, three floors, wrap around porch, pretty curtains, and flower boxes. Her seven-year-old-self wanted to cry—this was what she had dreamed of on all those cold, hungry nights. Her thirty-one-year-old self, approved. As did Mia, who clapped her chubby little hands.

The house was impressive, like its owner. However, broad shoulders, powerful thighs, and a face that would stop traffic—*and rugged enough to hint that maybe he had done that a time or two*—did not, necessarily make a good father.

Although, much as she didn't want to admit it, she could see why Hope had fallen for him. She shrugged. Thankfully she wasn't Hope, and it would take a heck of a lot more than a cute face and hot body to crack through her defenses.

Moving up the steps, each one bearing pots of colorful flowers at each side, flipped her thoughts in another direction; gave her pause… Could the investigative report have been wrong? Could there be a Mrs. JD Halligan? There was a definite female vibe going on here, which might pose a problem she hadn't considered. Sighing, she continued her perusal. Several groups of cane seating were placed at various intervals along the wide deck, along with two swing seats. While in good condition, they looked like they'd been there forever, every one boasted brightly colored cushions, some with contrasting bobble edging. Whoever had designed this had a good eye.

But perhaps not a good ear, not if her repeated unsuccessful attempts to have someone answer the door were any example. He'd slammed the screened door but, spurred on by building frustration and worry about standing outside in the cooling air with the baby, she eventually discovered he hadn't locked it. Opening it just wide enough to poke her head in, she called into the wide foyer, her gaze stretching along the lengthy passageway. "Mr. Halligan? JD? Please, we need to talk."

More silence.

Evie glanced down at Mia, meeting the child's now solemn-eyed stare, the one that seemed to see so much. Perhaps she'd be a philosopher? "I know, baby," she said, pausing to feather a light kiss on Mia's forehead. "But, hey, maybe the scary man isn't as bad as he seems."

Or maybe he is, an inner voice countered.

She couldn't stand there all night. The cooling air, desperation and weariness won out over manners, and she boldly stepped into the house. Mia had cried for the entire flight from San Francisco to Bozeman, only settling once they were in the rental car. Added to her own recent lack of sleep, Evie had been exhausted, and the drive had almost finished her off. Yet, now she had to contend with a rude, bullheaded cowboy. Well, she was in the right mood to take him on...

The thick carpet runner swallowed her footsteps as she tentatively moved deeper into the house, passing by the staircase, calling out at every other step.

Several rooms led off the long, generous corridor. Darted glances revealed each space furnished for comfort and family living. Soft plump sofas, wing chairs pulled up to fireplaces that sat ready for the changing weather, overfilled bookcases, ottomans slightly bent out of shape from frequent use, a table that accommodated at least twelve diners...

The care instruction leaflets for this furniture probably didn't show a child's image crossed through. They possibly even featured that image in a heart-shape. Dogs too.

Those half-forgotten childhood dreams resurfaced again. *So, this is what a real home looked like.* A home... Was this the life Mia would have if JD Halligan accepted his responsibility?

Mia started to fuss. "Shh, hang on baby. Not yet." Evie wasn't taking chances in case that hypothetical dog really existed.

The hallway opened up to a massive kitchen and family room, which like the rest of the house, was ominously quiet. Obviously, a more recent addition, it also boasted a staircase leading to the upper floors. Evie wasn't much of a cook—not a cook at all—but even she could tell the kitchen was a homemaker's delight. Yet no delicious aromas wafted in the air, no pots bubbled on the stovetop.

The open-plan family room area beyond housed more of that same comfortable furniture, with framed photographs lining the walls and settled on flat surfaces. A true family room and she imagined a rowdy family gathered there, teasing and laughing… Children running around.

But there was no family gathered, rowdy or otherwise. And it seemed—wrong, somehow. Only the combined hum of the refrigerator and a heating unit saved it from being morgue-quiet.

She glanced up the stairs. Should she? If he wasn't down here then surely that's where he'd be? Mia began fussing again, this time waving her arms, her little face scrunched and red. Flicking her wrist Evie checked the time. "You're hungry? Of course, you are. Well," she said, sparing one more glance up the stairs, "I guess whatever goes up, has to come down. How about we wait it out? And in the meantime, you can have some milk and a snack. Sound good?"

Nineteen minutes later there had still been no sign of JD Halligan, and Evie's temper was stretched about as fine as it could without completely snapping. Obviously, he hadn't believed her story—not that he'd given her the opportunity to explain—but still, surely manners decreed he at least hear her out. One thing was certain, even if she had to camp out here all night, she wasn't leaving until they'd talked.

And the sooner that happened the better.

One option presented itself immediately and before she stopped to rationalize her decision, she walked straight to the staircase.

A matching runner to the carpet in the corridor protected the stairs and with Mia settled on her hip she made her way to the next floor. Once more, several doors opened off the passage that ran both right and left. Most doors were closed, however one down on the far right was ajar. Calling his name once more, she strode to that door, knocking lightly, and then pushing it gently as she again called out her intention to enter.

Bare feet dangling over the edge of the bed should have been her warning but her head was so full of other things that it missed the memo. Thankfully, despite her determination, her steps were tentative, cautious… Just one step into that gloom, one step over the threshold.

But that was enough. Way, way enough.

Chapter Two

Her squeal startled Mia who responded with a squeal of her own that immediately built into a full-volume howl.

In turn, the pseudo domino effect triggered the naked man lying on the bed to jackknife into a sitting position. "W-wha...?" Eyes heavy with sleep blinked once, twice, maybe three times. Then his indignant roar hit the air at the exact same time his hands landed heavily to protect his manhood.

Rousing herself from her shock, Evie's one free hand was rapidly alternating between covering her own eyes and covering Mia's. "*Don't look, don't look, don't look...*" The repetitive mutter wasn't helping. Refusing to be pacified or close her eyes, Mia's little fists dragged at Evie's hand, determined not to have her eyes covered. *Hussy!*

Giving up, she snapped her own eyes closed. "What are you doing?"

"What am *I* doing? What are *you* doing in my bedroom?"

"You're naked!"

"Yes! Because it's *my* bedroom!"

She opened one eye. It was just as bad—or good—as the image in her head.

He made to move, paused, snatched up a pillow that he placed strategically, then rose to stride toward her, his intention clear. At least she *hoped* he was only going to close the door.

He did. Evie backtracked, moving Mia out of harm's way just before the door slammed shut in their faces. Cheeks burning with embarrassment, she once more took to the stairs. She'd have run if she hadn't been carrying Mia.

One thing was clear. Embarrassed or not, she was not leaving until he came back down. Fully clothed.

Actually, two things were clear. The second one defiantly refused to be erased from memory. She tried. But like... *He needed a pillow? A whole pillow?*

And why was she focused on that? It was exhaustion. It had to be. It had weakened her. Made her vulnerable. She never reacted to men this way. She always coolly assessed. She never just *reacted*!

She'd barely made it to the family room when he reappeared—bare feet, clean jeans, and a black T-shirt he was still pulling on over that impressive sun-browned chest. Very impressive chest. *Stop! She commanded silently.*

She looked down. And saw that butt—very neatly encased in those soft, hugging jeans.

No, no, no... She looked back up; made herself focus on

his face. And of course *that* didn't help one bit.

Even with a scowl he was even better looking without the hat, and a flash of heat burned through her when she recalled *again* exactly how *much* of him, she'd seen. His hair, she now discovered, was a dirty blonde color, sandy, and a bit scruffy. It went perfectly with his sun-browned skin. She'd expected blue or gray eyes with that coloring but his were as dark and delicious as…as…

As Mia's.

The realization slammed hard in her chest and her heart suddenly felt heavier. Had she been hoping this man wasn't actually Mia's father? Hoping he hadn't cavalierly had a quick affair and waltzed on without a backward glance?

But why?

If that was indeed the case, if he truly *wasn't* Mia's father, then she'd have to revert to Plan B, the one she was astutely ignoring. *Though*, that perpetually annoying little voice she'd developed since she'd first taken Mia in her arms whispered, *even if he is her father, it doesn't mean you're leaving Mia with him. What if he's unsuitable?*

It was true. Evie had known in her heart of hearts from the beginning that she would never, *could never*, leave Mia, *any child*, with someone who wouldn't safely care for her; who wouldn't love her—no matter how much inner panic it caused within herself.

So far, he hadn't said a word. Casting a lazy glance across to where Evie sat—uninvited—on one of the plump sofa chairs, with Mia playing at her feet, JD Halligan continued straight to the kitchen area. Sighed. And finally got to the point. His point. "I thought I asked you to leave my property. I should have you arrested for breaking and entering."

The words sounded fierce but Evie noted more weariness in that gravelly tone than acrimony, and a sliver of empathy diluted the sting in her own response. "There was no breaking. You left the door unlatched."

He maintained his calm. "Unlatched but closed. Most people are aware of what that signifies. There's also a welcome message on the doormat, but that doesn't mean it gives people cart-blanche to traipse in at will."

"*Most* people wouldn't leave a woman and baby standing on their front porch, either. Especially a woman and baby who had traveled over a thousand miles to get here."

She caught the quick frown. The narrowing of his eyes as he digested that statement. "And *most people*," he countered, "wouldn't travel a thousand miles and not warn someone they were coming."

"*Most people* would. Agreed. And I did. I left a message."

That stopped him. "When?"

"Two days ago."

Frowning, he appeared to reach for a cell phone, stalling when she clarified. "Landline. I didn't have a cell number."

His head dropped back, and his eyes closed momentarily as he rolled over this extra information—slotted it into place "Storm." He sighed again, opened his eyes and headed toward the king-sized refrigerator. "Knocked out our power, phone connections. I haven't checked it since it was reinstated."

"You haven't checked your phone in two days?" Incredulity underpinned every word.

"Lady, I—" He shook his head, swiped a hand across his face, and pulled open the fridge door. "I need a bee—" Pausing, he flicked a glance back across to his two unexpected guests and closed the fridge door. Maybe there'd been another sigh. *"Coffee."*

Making an about-face he reached for two mugs, pointing one in her direction. She nodded and he indicated the baby with another flick of his head. "What about…? Would she?"

Straight-faced, Evie blinked once, slowly. *"She* is Mia, and *she* has currently sworn off both—beer and coffee. Perhaps when she turns one…"

Amusement twinkled in his eyes for a mere moment before he turned to fill the water tank of the coffee machine. "Mia? Okay… And you are?"

She cleared her throat. "Evie. Evie Davis."

"Well *Evie*, I meant would she—*Mia*—like water, or milk, or maybe juice?"

Against her will, her own lips melted into a smile. "Thank you, but she's fine. She just had a snack."

Other than ask for her coffee preference, he said nothing more until he dropped heavily into a sofa chair next to hers. At their feet, and on her tummy, the baby played happily with the toys Evie had pulled out of the oversized baby bag she'd lugged all the way from San Francisco. Right then Mia was gnawing furiously on the ear of a baby-safe rubber bunny rabbit, paying them no attention.

Lifting the mug he'd placed on the coffee table between them, Evie nodded her thanks before breaking the silence. "JD, Mr. Halligan? I suggest we get this over with as quickly and painlessly as possible. I'm not sure how long that bunny will keep her interest."

"Ma'am, I'm trying to be civil here, trying to display the manners my mother hammered into me, but I meant what I said outside. Now, if this truly isn't some kind of prank, then I'm afraid you're in for a big disappointment. There is no way I am this child's father."

IT WAS AS though speaking the word triggered the emotion because he swore he saw disappointment shadow those clear blue eyes. Which, in itself was a crying shame because they were probably the prettiest eyes he'd ever seen. In this light, they were more aqua than plain blue, and so clear and bright. Intelligent. Hell, if he was being honest, that wasn't the only pretty thing about her—under other circumstances he'd consider her to be the whole package, physically at least, but right then it was her eyes that held him.

He was also certain that if he'd ever had relations with this woman, he'd have definitely remembered.

That prompted the other obvious question. Surely, she'd known he couldn't have fathered her child? She didn't look like the sort of woman who would forget something like that. Yet, she hadn't immediately recognized him. So, what was he missing?

"Hey... Ah, look, maybe we got off on the wrong foot back there an—"

"*You* got off on the wrong foot, Mr. Halligan. My feet were firmly planted, precisely as they are now."

He couldn't help it, and anyway, *anyone* would have done the same thing. Word association. He flicked a glance down at her feet—tanned, petite, with pink toes that peeped out from the front of those ridiculously high heels. His pulse kicked up a beat and he jerked his head up, forcing his gaze... Anywhere but at her. *What? He was getting off on feet now?* Snatching up his mug, he swallowed the contents in one gulp, lurching forward in his chair when the scalding coffee burned a trail right down to his gut.

Evie Davis stretched one hand across toward him. "Are you okay?"

Obviously not. Any sense he'd possessed before this woman had waltzed into his house had somehow deserted him. He put it down to exhaustion.

And hunger.

He wanted to tell her he was fine, to just forget it. To move on and get out of there so he could regain his equilibrium. Instead, he mumbled, *"Who wears heels to a ranch anyway?"*

Which only made it all worse.

"Pardon?" Her eyes widened, and he hoped the question he saw there indicated she hadn't really heard.

"Ahhh... Dinner. I was thinking about dinner."

"*Now?*" Her tone was incredulous. Just as it should be. "I mean, it's only," she glanced at the fancy wristwatch, the bulkiness of the wide white band accentuating the slenderness of her wrist, "four-thirty but—*now?*"

Only four-thirty? *So much for diversions.* He needed to move. Maybe it would get the blood flowing back to his brain. Pitching to his feet, he strode to the kitchen island, dumped the mug, turned, and leaned back against the cool granite. Arms crossed, he once more gave her his focus. "Yeah, you're right. I don't know what I was thinking." Scraping his hand down over his face he offered a grin. "I guess this is what you get when you drop in on a guy who's had about six hours sleep in the past forty-eight." One hand lifted in a lazy wave. "So, go ahead, say your piece, and then we can get this settled."

Evie stared at him for long enough for him to start to worry that something even worse was headed his way than had already been thrown at him. The frown reappeared, and her mouth had scrunched into a pout that emphasized those soft full lips.

He hauled in air; refolded his arms. Man, he really needed to eat. Or sleep. Something.

Finally, that clear, well-modulated voice addressed him. "Are you married, Mr. Halligan? Children?" He shook his head and she moved on. "Good." The last word arrived in a whispered rush, and he wondered at the sudden rosy flush that—*heaven forbid*—even made that pretty face even more gorgeous. Wondered more at the accompanying flash of panic he'd caught in her eyes before they darted away, down to her feet. Drawing his attention back to where this all started. He was doomed. *Oh man...*

She didn't lift her eyes as she continued, but he determinedly lifted his own. "I ah... I mean, I've been told that Mia's father is a good man; that he—"

That sobered him. "You don't know? You didn't work that out for yourself?"

"I'm sorry, I don't see how I could have done that..."

It was his turn to be incredulous. His eyes automatically slipped to the baby. "Well, surely you formed some kind of an opinion when..." He broke off, letting his raised eyebrows fill in the rest.

"When what?"

He almost laughed. "Like, when she was conceived for starters."

It was too much. He'd gone too far and her tightly held features left him in no doubt as to how much too far. "Perhaps I don't know because I wasn't *at* her conception." She waited a beat. "And that could possibly be because *I am not Mia's mother*."

The last words were enunciated slowly, firmly, leaving no room for misunderstanding—and unwanted relief rushed through him that he hadn't been wrong about sleeping with this woman. Because somehow, he figured it would've been a standout.

"Where's the mother?"

"She's … um, she's very ill. Too unwell to care for her child right now."

Eyes narrowed, he said, "So, you're telling me that you're not this baby's mama. And I'm telling you I'm not her father. So, do you mind telling me what in the hell is going on? Just what we're doing here?" The obvious answer slid into place, bringing with it a nasty taste he had difficulty identifying. Once more his eyes went to the baby, noting the satin soft wisps of hair, the soft, reddish blonde curls on the very top that were so damned cute. "You're social services or something?"

"Or something." She sighed. "JD—can I call you that?" At his nod she continued, her voice calm, her tone soft. "I'm afraid I have documentation here that indicates that you really are Mia's father. Everything on this birth certificate, name, address, occupation—it's all you."

Moving back to her, he stretched out one hand. "May I…"

Having been told what it would contain, he needed little more than a glance to satisfy his curiosity, handing the sheet of paper back to her with a shake of his head. He wasn't

Mia's father, he knew that for sure. However, that didn't mean someone else in the family couldn't be the father. But it also could be some kind of deliberate misdirection, and until they knew more, it was his duty to protect his family. "Look, I know what you want this to prove, but really? It means nothing. Anyone could have used this name while they were—involved—with Mia's mother." He sighed. "I'm sorry, but you'd need more proof than this."

CONFUSION SWEPT IN on a wave. Could Hope have been wrong? But, there *really* was a JD Halligan of Marietta, Montana—of the Lazy H Ranch, so? Or was his theory the right one? Had someone lied to Hope? Used a false name? If that was the truth then it obviously had to be someone who knew of this man. But, why would they do that? Why not fabricate a name rather than pilfer one?

Evie stared up at him, her mind turning over all these questions. Over the years she'd developed a reasonably accurate BS barometer. Occupational advantage. And on the surface, it would be so easy to generalize, to brand JD Halligan as a typical hot cowboy with a girl at every watering hole, barely remembering their names—because he certainly wouldn't be short of women ready to throw themselves at him.

And yet that BS barometer was being decidedly quiet. Which meant, what? That lack of sleep had made her lose her touch? Or that he was as sincere as he appeared?

His eyes narrowed as he returned her gaze. "Surely you didn't expect the father, whoever he is, to simply accept your assumption?" His tone was gentle. "Or that piece of paper?"

She dragged in air, forcing herself back to the present. "I admit I expected this conversation to go down very differently." The surprise in his eyes prompted her to add, "And *I*, especially, should have known better. However, Hope—Hope Reynolds—Mia's mother, seemed so adamant, so convinced not only of the identity of Mia's father, but that he would want to care for his daughter. It led me to believe there was a deep understanding between them. And I shouldn't have just accepted that as fact."

"Perhaps there was—*is*—a deep understanding," he said softly. "It just wasn't with *me*."

"So, I guess there's no way to convince you to take a paternity test?"

Once more he raked a hand down over his face. "Evie? Can I…?" She nodded, trying to ignore how her name rolled off his tongue, how it kind of rumbled across to her, seeming to close the gap between them. And completely unable to ignore the sincerity she saw in those burnt-caramel eyes. "If," he continued, "it brought an end to all this, then I'd be happy to do so for your sake as well as mine, but that's gonna take time and time is something I'm in mighty short supply of right now. And would only prove what I'm trying to tell you."

"I think all I'd need is your consent and maybe a hair sample. Maybe a mouth swab."

One dark eyebrow rose, like a prefix to his question. "That would prove she has Halligan blood? Or not…?"

"And, just for argument's sake, if it did? *Did* prove she was a Halligan?"

"Okay." He sighed. "For argument's sake only, if it did, it poses another problem. I'm, *we're*, in no position to care for a child right now." He held up his hands as though to ward off an attack. "If she is a Halligan, she would be accepted with open arms—but it doesn't change the current practicalities."

Evie frowned. "I understood that your parents lived nearby?" She looked around. "Here, even?"

He didn't question her knowledge source. "They live in town. Moved there a year or so ago—and they're currently away on an extended trip."

"Oh, I see…" She had no idea what this meant. It was totally alien of her not to have considered every possibility, yet, this time she hadn't. Hadn't considered anything apart from the obvious. She was still mulling over her lack of foresight when Mia suddenly emitted a blood-curdling scream. Diving out of the chair, Evie reached for the crying baby, heart pounding as her eyes searched frantically for a reason, for something to have bitten or hurt her. Tucking Mia's head into her shoulder, panic set in as she rocked the baby back and forth.

JD was at her side in an instant, concern wreathing his face, his eyes following the path Evie's had taken, searching the floor. "I can't see anything that might have—"

"Me either." The breathlessness in her voice brought his gaze straight back to her.

"Are you okay? What do you want me to do? Does she need a doctor?"

Unexpected tears stung her eyes, which she again blamed on exhaustion. "I don't know," she said, raising her voice to be heard over the noise. "She's never screamed like that before. YouTube didn't cover that…"

"YouTube?" Yes, there was definite incredulity in his voice.

"What?" Again, her voice rose up over the baby's howls, as Evie frantically jiggled to try to pacify her. "You're judging me? Really? So how else was I supposed to learn what to do!"

"Wait," he said, disbelief now underpinning every word, he too yelling over Mia's cries. "Someone let you bring a baby halfway across the country with your only experience being *YouTube*?"

Indignation pooled in her shoulders which momentarily straightened. "Excuse me? It was thirteen and half hours of intense viewing and note-taking! Thirteen and half hours I could have slept, but no, I spent that time learning as much as I could." She jiggled a bit more fervently, frustrated sarcasm bubbling on her tongue. "Obviously the episode that covered this situation must have been for those who signed up for fourteen hours!" The jiggling increased in intensity.

His mouth twitched. "Obviously." Placing a gentle hand on her shoulder, he added. "Evie?" It took a second attempt to reach her. "Evie? I think you can dial back the rocking a bit. She's stopped crying."

His tone had been as gentle as his touch. "Oh. Right..." It was true Mia was now snuffling into Evie's shoulder.

His eyes were kind as he glanced down at the baby and then back to Evie. Holding out his hands he said, "Maybe if I...? Maybe we can figure out what went wrong."

Like on replay, she once more simply said, "Oh," as he carefully took the baby from her arms, a reassuring smile on his face as he turned the tot to him.

Her little face immediately scrunched as though ready to cry again, and JD surprised Evie by holding Mia tight against him, soothing the baby, whose tiny fists stopped waving for long enough for him to inspect her arms.

His gaze moved up and he was first to spot the teeny specks of blood around her mouth. He was also the only one of the two adults who didn't fall apart. Long tanned fingers, tenderly moved Mia's lower lip, smiling as he turned to Evie. "I think she just popped a tooth. We should have guessed. She was giving that rabbit a pretty hard time."

Feeling both relieved and slightly embarrassed, she nodded. "Hope said she was tee—" She pulled up short. Still in JD's arms Mia was settled now; settled and bestowing on him that steady, solemn-eyed-stare that seemed to carry the wisdom of the ages. It was JD's reaction to it, though, that had stalled Evie's speech. "Is something wrong?"

He said nothing. Was it possible his face had paled? Or was it a trick of the light? One thing she didn't have to wonder about was his sudden dazed expression, or how those eyes had, almost impossibly, darkened in the past few seconds.

Finally, he spoke, his tone grim. "You'd better take her." It was all he said before he handed over the baby and turned back to the kitchen, this time snatching up the beer he'd denied himself earlier. "I'll go haul all that stuff in."

Chapter Three

Several hours later, JD eyed the brother who'd casually walked through the house. Too casually. Cattleman's hat dangling from his fingers. And suddenly that steak he'd just downed was giving him indigestion. Not that it needed much help. He'd had to force down every mouthful, and only then because he knew he needed to keep his strength up to complete all the work that needed doing. "If you're lookin' for food—"

"Nah, already ate." Jack flicked him a distracted grin, his eyes everywhere but on his big brother, resting curiously for a long moment, on the pile of baby paraphernalia. "Haven't been out here for a while. Thought I'd check in."

"Yeah?" JD bent to put the last of the dishes in the dishwasher and hit the Start button. "Hey, you know I heard about this new-fangled device—called a telephone. Just saying…"

Jack's gaze moved to the stairs, frowning as it traveled upward. "Yeah? Maybe I'll try that sometime. Might even work if you ever bothered to answer it."

Ignoring the jibe, JD leaned back against the counter and

watched his brother, feigning innocence as he said, "Looking for something, bro?"

Jack finally gave his brother his attention, the droop of his shoulders signaling defeat. "She's not here, is she?"

Again, JD assumed an expression he hoped was a picture of oblivion. *"She?"*

Jack's sigh was echoed by the thump of his hat hitting the granite counter top. "Oh, come on, man! You know exactly what I'm talking about. It's all over town."

JD winced. "Let me guess. A smart-mouthed truck driver?"

"Yup. He called in at Greys, happily entertaining all assembled about the funniest story he'd come across as a driver, apparently." He paused. "Is it true? You've got a kid? Mom's gonna flip her wig—her dream come true. But at least it'll get her to back off on the rest of us for a while."

It was JD's turn to sigh. "Don't get too far ahead of yourself, bro." Turning to the fridge he snagged two beers and nodded toward the sofa. "You'd better brace yourself." He flicked a quick glance up the stairwell. "And keep your voice down."

"She *is* here? It's true?"

"*She* and the baby are up in the guest room. And don't give me that phony all-righteous look—the folks would have done the same thing, and you know it."

Maybe he did but Jack hadn't needed words to express his opinion of both that decision and his big brother—it was written all over his face. None of it complimentary.

Normally that would simply wash over him, but tonight his brother's opinion rankled, and JD's clipped response lobbed a counter-judgment over the net. "The baby was fussing, wouldn't settle, so *Evie* prepared to leave, had a room all booked at Bramble House but remembered too late that she hadn't organized a crib—more to the point she was dead on her feet. It would have been dangerous for her to drive into town, and I'd had a couple of beers." He shrugged. "There was a crib here—courtesy of the mouthy truck driver—so I set it up while she bathed and fed the little one. End of story."

Sort of...

After finding some linen that could be used for the crib and a soft throw that his grandmother had crafted, JD had let Evie get on with whatever she'd had to do, only worrying when considerable time had passed. That's when he'd checked in and found her on the bed, wrapped in the robe he'd offered, and like the baby, sound asleep. She'd pulled the crib close to the bed and one hand was stretched through the side rails, stretched out far enough for her fingers to be lightly clasped around Mia's.

Evie's hair had been down and loose, a soft, golden wave that washed down over her shoulder, and he'd itched to lift back the stray strands that had fallen partway across her face. Even partially covered, and even in sleep, her exhaustion was evident, exhaustion that still failed to camouflage her delicate beauty. Had caring for Mia been the cause? And he wondered again why it was she, of all people, who was tasked with bringing Mia to his family.

Suddenly, feeling like some creepy voyeur, he'd backed out, but that image had come with him.

That had been over an hour ago, but that image stayed, front and center. Meanwhile his brother waited, but forcing his mind away from Evie was tougher than JD had imagined and he was becoming irritated with himself that he was allowing her to take up so much space in his head.

Relaying the story—as he knew it—to his brother didn't help that situation but it did redirect his thoughts to the real reason for all this upheaval—a Halligan baby, a child... His family would have him strung up if he didn't follow through and get to the bottom of this. But when? How? All this couldn't have happened at a worse time. Responsibility weighed in heavily but the devil on his shoulder wasn't suckered in, posing the question of why he was taking it all on himself, of why he wasn't batting some of it back to Jack?

Deliberately ignoring that voice, he finished the story realizing as he did, exactly how many holes still needed to be filled.

So, it seemed, did Jack. "So, it's a scam? Has to be..." His eyes narrowed as he tried to make sense of what he'd just heard. "If this kid isn't yours...?"

JD inhaled, deep and long, his head dropping back against the sofa as he blew it back out. "Not mine, but"—he paused, turned to face his brother; his tone somber—"I'm pretty sure she's a Halligan. She's got the eye." When Jack continued to stare, he clarified, "The birthmark."

Jack's hand shot to his own face and then dropped away just as fast. Both he and their younger brother, Julian—a.k.a. *Leo*, shared the unusual eye marking with their paternal grandmother. At a quick glance it simply looked like one iris was bigger than the other, like someone had colored outside the lines on one side—a marking so unusual it was considered rare.

And for once, the man proven to be the joker of the family didn't seem to be able to find anything funny to say. "Hell, one of us really is a daddy?" Shadows now clouded those distinctive eyes. "So, how old is this baby?"

"About six months. Just shy of it according to Evie." Raising both eyebrows, JD held his brother's gaze. "Don't suppose you were out San Francisco way about fifteen, sixteen months ago?"

There was a heartbeat before Jack responded, every word carried on a wave of quiet shock. "Hell, I don't even know..."

"The name Hope doesn't ring a bell? Hope Reynolds?"

"Hope?" Jack's eyes searched the ceiling before returning to JD. "Sorry, man." He shook his head, his shoulders lifting ever so slightly as he spoke. "Hey, look, it's not like it hasn't ever happened but I'm not really the one-night-stand kinda guy." One eyebrow zoomed north as JD's snort called him out. "Yeah, yeah, okay… But not for a few years, at least. That was then. Not now. What I'm trying to say is that if the name doesn't mean anything to me then it sorta indicates it was a pretty brief hook-up, so, on that basis only, it might rule me out." JD's mouth opened and Jack raised both hands. "I say *might,* okay? What did she say when you told her?"

A frisson of discomfort slithered through JD. "The thing is, I haven't exactly done that yet." He held up a hand to ward off any criticism that may be headed his way. "I know, I know… To be honest I was kinda rocked when I saw the baby's eye, and so much stuff started shooting around in my head. I wanted a minute to think it through, but then she was tied up with the baby, and then she fell asleep and I—"

"Well, I think you kinda blew it man, but, I can't say I'd have been any more clear-headed. It would have been a shock—actually *is* a shock." He shrugged. "So, *Evie,* huh? Sounds cozy… Heard she's pretty hot."

Jack's rapid topic change didn't surprise JD, he knew his brother well enough to know he'd need to get his thoughts in order privately, but he wasn't prepared for the twist in his gut when that new topic came. The instant image it brought… Of that face, those eyes, the cute pout he was certain she was unaware accentuated her soft, full lips—an image that brought with it an equally instant rush of heat making a determined beeline in the direction of south. A pooling of heat that the base of his still cold beer bottle was useless to divert.

Holding up a hand was as much a warning to himself as to his brother. "You can stop right there, buddy. Yeah, okay, I'll admit she's tempting, but that's not a road I want to go down again."

When she'd assumed she'd be leaving, Evie had handed over her business card so he'd have her number. *Evelyn Davis*—not social services—but the fact she was a lawyer hadn't really surprised him either. Still, he'd looked up the law firm on his phone… Fancy. Big hitters. Which meant she was probably a big hitter herself, or on the way there. Personally, he had nothing against big city business women, but he'd learned the hard way that they and ranch life didn't mix well.

Jack's voice pulled him back to the present. "What? You're not still beating yourself up over Samantha, are you? Geez, man—that was over two years ago. If you ask me, you had a lucky escape! She was all wrong for you." His frown formed an incredulous V-shape as another thought formed. "Hell, is that why you know this baby isn't yours?" He whistled, the sound echoing through the large room. "Two years? What are you? A monk?"

The face of the mouthy truck driver flashed into his head. "Apparently I'm the only one not seeing a problem here…" JD muttered. Clearing his voice, he said, "Shut it down, bro. I don't tell you how to live your life—and not that it's any of your business, but I haven't exactly taken a vow of celibacy. I just haven't met anybody..." He stopped. Stopped before his mouth offered what his head was thinking. *Until now.* Because even thinking it was a very bad move. He didn't need to say it out loud as well.

Jack simply shrugged. "Whatever—but what are you going to do about the baby?"

JD shrugged in return. "Talk to Leo—then go from there. If you're not playing dodgeball here, then that puts Leo well and truly in the frame." Thoughts were lining up almost faster than he could get a handle on them. "I dunno if that means we still have to take tests but it'd probably be a wasted effort—unless to prove a family relationship in case Leo doesn't get here soon." Evie's arrival had pushed his exhaustion to the side, but responsibility weighed heavy. "I get that as a family, we're responsible, but it's put us in a bit of a jam. Thing is, I get the feeling Evie expects to leave the baby with us, but with Mom and Dad away for another three or four months and Doreen off on that cruise with her sister, Leo somewhere out on the circuit—and the herd..."

Jack nodded. "When's Doreen due back?"

"A bit over three weeks. After the cruise they're heading down to New Mexico to meet up with some long-lost relatives." The faithful housekeeper had been with the family for more than twenty-five years, and there was no way JD was going to spoil this trip by asking her to come back. Or his mom. Both those women deserved their break, especially their mom—it was her first proper vacation in thirty-seven years. When their dad had his heart attack he'd finally agreed to sell up to JD and move into town where they could enjoy more time with their friends, and this European trip was the beginning of the rest of their new lives.

"Joey?"

JD shook his head. "Nah, she's got enough on her plate." Anyway, of all the siblings, their sister was obviously the one with the least skin in this particular game. Literally.

Pulling himself to his feet, JD stared down at his brother, who stood to face him. There was next to nothing in height difference or build and with only a little over four years separating all three brothers, they'd not only been a formidable force for their parents as youngsters, but all firm friends as well.

"So, it's us, then." Jack stretched out his hand to clasp JD's shoulder. "I could rock, paper, scissors you to decide who gets to babysit, but how about I offer to take over the herd while you sort this? I know a couple of guys who might help out." Perhaps sensing a protest brewing, he rushed on, "Good guys, JD; reliable. They're finished over on the Callaghan property."

JD could have argued, after all, even if he'd assured his siblings they'd all always have a home there if needed, ultimately, this was *his* ranch now. The fact that he didn't—*argue*—worried him. Worried him just as much as the fact that his heart had literally leaped at the thought of spending more time with Evie. And his niece of course. *But, with*

Evie...

And that was an all-out bad idea.

Especially when the answer to the question he'd asked himself several minutes earlier hit him with the force of an airborne boulder. Why hadn't he passed over some of the responsibility to Jack? *Because he didn't want to...*

Hell yeah... *Bad, bad, bad...*

JD noted his brother's eyes again narrowed when his sigh had been long and deep, and he cleared his throat to cover up anymore unwanted speculation. "Yeah, might work. I'll come down with you all tomorrow, get you set up."

˜

EVIE COULDN'T BLAME her surroundings. The Halligan guest room, complete with adjoining bathroom, had lived up to everything she'd already noted—and fantasized—about this house. Cozy and comfortable, cared for. Its autumnal color scheme with the surprising dusky pink accents worked well, and paired perfectly with furniture that had history and bore the odd scratch with pride. Under other circumstances this room would no doubt deliver a sense of peace and calm. So, no, the accommodation hadn't been the problem. And this time Evie couldn't even completely blame the gurgling little imp currently propped up between a mountain of pillows on the floor—for her own restless night.

Not that sleep had ever come easily. Even without the extraordinary circumstances of the past several days, Evie didn't usually have to look far for things to keep her awake at night. Residual habits left from her unstable childhood meant she collected them like others collected seashells or coffee mugs—*randomly*. Her current catalogue though, was extreme even by her own standards. Her concern for baby Mia and this situation topped the list, added to worry about Hope's condition and progress, her current case at work—even crazy incidental things like the occasional flashed memory of the woman she'd seen on the side of the road right outside of town as she'd driven past. Something about that scene hadn't sat well with her at the time, and typically, even *that* should have played havoc with her attempted rest. It was the way her head worked, and at any other time, any and all of those would have been fighting for her attention.

Not this time.

No, the fact that Evie had barely slept a wink had to be placed right at the abs—um, feet—of a certain dark-eyed rancher; the fact that he had been sleeping just down the hall was not helping at all.

Actually, that wasn't precisely true. She *had* slept. *Some.* She remembered getting Mia off to sleep, and thinking she'd rest for only a moment. However, when she'd woken at near midnight, her slightly refreshed head had performed a replay of everything that had gone down since she'd arrived. And then replayed the highlights over and over, somehow continuing to get snagged on that sun-browned face, the jaw, those lips. Oh yeah, those lips… Those—*stop!* All those—*things*—

needed to be packed away in a big sturdy box with the word TROUBLE written across the top. JD Halligan was one big sidetrack she could not afford.

She'd noted his upturned mug on the sink when she'd ventured down earlier to get Mia's breakfast—the problem being she'd noticed; had looked for him; wondered about him. *Big sidetrack.* And all more reasons to put an end to these schoolgirl reactions by getting this paternity issue settled today and make plans to get back to work.

Momentarily closing her eyes, she drew in a long slow breath, calmed herself. She just had to maintain focus.

JD Halligan was more than an unexpected distraction; he was a *force*—the likes of which she hadn't experienced since… Ever. But she was also confident enough to believe she could control the situation. Wasn't that what she did every day? What had made her so successful, so far? Her ability to maintain control?

As if she needed a reminder of where her priorities should lay, her phone chirped another message from her assistant who needed clarity about something for the case she was working on. Anxiety gnawed at her as she tapped out her response; she was already behind with her work. The D'Alessio case had been a gift, the one that would cement her place at the firm and hopefully go a long way to assure her of the partnership she was hoping to secure before she was forty. Closer to fulfilling the dream she'd held close since she'd first been offered her current position—not for the prestige—but for the security she'd craved since she'd first understood what that word meant; what it represented.

Closing her eyes again, Evie took a moment to visualize her dream board—the inspirational quotes, the daily mantras. Over the years her dreams had changed, matured, but that desire for stability, security, had always been her mainstay.

It'd carried her through childhood, through holding down three jobs while at college, and it still carried her through her career.

And it would carry her through this detour and keep her on track.

Mia offered her opinion of that with a *grizzle*, drawing Evie's attention. The baby's chubby legs pumped while determined little fists rubbed at her eyes, and immediately Evie scooped her up, pressed her lips to the satin soft cheek. "Hey baby girl. You're tired?" Mia responded by nuzzling into Evie's shoulder, her eyelids heavy. "You are?" she whispered, "Hey, we're getting better at this communication thing, yeah?"

Blessedly it took only minutes for Mia to drop off, but several more before Evie could bring herself to put the baby in the crib. Finally tiptoeing away, she settled into an easy chair, intending to deal with the pile of emails that had accumulated over the past day but her eyes kept straying to the baby, watching the rise and fall of her little chest. Mesmerized by the rosebud mouth that occasionally bunched then relaxed. Inhaling the peace that had descended around them, cocooning them in this pretty room.

Focusing on work was an unaccustomed effort, and not even a reminder of its importance helped get her head into place. Nothing worked. Closing her eyes, she fought for perspective: Mia would be in her life fleetingly—Evie's *own* life, her own goals, dreams, plans, were back in San Francisco. And she couldn't lose sight of that.

On a sigh she determinedly turned back to her laptop, managing to reply to only one office query before the blast from her phone shattered that silence, that peace—and Mia's sleep. And she managed to convey all the subsequent frustration into one word, *"What?"*

Chapter Four

F OR A MOMENT there was nothing. Silence.
Then, "Bad time?"

That voice... *His voice...* Gravelly, sliding seductively along her nerve ends. She sighed, hating that it had taken just two words to threaten her resolve, prompting her to visualize herself sitting on that aforementioned box to keep it sealed as *that voice* rumbled over her. "Most people, knowing there's a baby in the house would consider the timing of a phone call. Common courtesy."

"And, *most people* who have a baby in their care would have their phone on vibrate. *Common sense.*"

Her eyes narrowed. Had she detected a note of smugness? Well, she was glad one of them was enjoying himself! "*Most* people have a reason for calling. Do you think we could get to yours?"

"And, *most* people have reasonable phone etiquette—but we'll let that pass. My reason? *Most* people eat breakfast, especially those who missed dinner. Besides, I thought you were the one in the big rush. I'm on my way back up to the house. I assumed you'd want to get started early to work this out."

He *was* enjoying this; she could hear it in his tone. "Well, unlike *most* people, right now I have a baby to calm down," she said, aiming for curt professionalism.

"So, that's a *yes*? I'll see you shortly."

And, oh how she wished for an old-fashioned phone she could slam into its cradle.

Despite Evie's own frustration, Mia didn't take long to settle back to sleep again. Snatching up the baby monitor she'd set up in the wee hours when it was obvious rest wouldn't come, she strode down the stairs, her stomach announcing her arrival with a loud gurgle she hoped he'd missed.

Fat chance, as his raised eyebrow and annoying grin clearly told her.

His eyes swept her from head to foot, and she added indignation to the arsenal of emotions he'd provoked in her. On the plus side, it was good to have something else to focus on that didn't include how her insides had betrayed her resolve by fluttering, annoyingly, as he'd made his obvious perusal. And she would not acknowledge the brief light that had shone from his eyes as they'd finally returned to her face. Would. Not.

She tightened her expression. "Surely even cowboys know this, but *most* people are not so blatantly rude."

He leaned lazily against the bank of cupboards, one long jeans-clad leg crossed over the other and his arms folded—

the frown his predominant expression. "I'm just thinking that *most people* don't wear a business suit to breakfast on a ranch."

"Oh…" Momentarily thrown off-kilter, she looked down at the pearl gray, raw silk-blend outfit, a clone of the style from yesterday, but this time the jacket was paired with a matching skirt. A short skirt… Her shoes were the same nude heels she'd worn since she'd arrived. The only ones she had with her. She felt heat traveling up her chest and higher, hoping it didn't make her appear as awkward as she suddenly felt. "You weren't just…?"

"Checking you out? Is that such a bad thing? You're a beautiful woman, so sure, I looked. But the outfit, classy as it is, still intrigues me. You didn't pack other, ah… you know, *less formal* clothes?"

Considering business attire was all she'd packed, it was pointless denying it. "Well, I guess I expected business meetings."

"Humph. So, this whole thing with Mia is just a business deal?"

There was no reproach, she'd give him that, but there was a flat ring in his tone that sounded a bit off. And she answered cautiously. "Well, no, of course not, but… Well, I had to pack quickly and—"

Comprehension lit his eyes, disbelief not far behind, and she swore she almost saw his mood change before her. "No way… Tell me this stuff isn't all you have in your wardrobe?" His laughter rang through the space and she knew she'd given herself away. "Really? Oh Evelyn, Evelyn, Evelyn... That's kinda sad. And I thought my life was a train wreck. What about when you're just bumming around? Or having fun?"

Count to ten. That's all she could do. *And breathe—don't forget to breathe...* When she'd controlled that, she spoke. Voice low, tone even. "It's *Evie* to you thank you very much—and... I beg your pardon? What right do y—"

Once more he interrupted her. "Breakfast?" he said cheerfully. He pointed to the toaster sitting beside a well-used pot and pan, and the array of food piled beside them. Bacon, eggs, tomatoes. "I didn't know how long you'd be and there's nothing worse than cold bacon and eggs, so I waited. I can do the bacon, save that pretty suit from getting all grease spattered. You want to do the eggs? I'll have whatever you're having. Omelet? Scrambled? Sunny-side up?"

She froze—unsure what had stunned her the most. The fact he could simply move on after insulting her?

Or the fact she was expected to cook?

Her heart sank. No, definitely the expectation that she could cook.

"Um, I..." *Are boiled eggs an option?* Possibly not. Which meant her repertoire was exhausted. She forced authority into her voice, pulled in air to push down the panic. "Or, we go with Plan B and I do the toast." Stepping forward with feigned bravado, she headed for the toaster. "I'm known for being able to brown a mean slice of bread."

JD frowned. "You don't want eggs? We can do something else. What's your specialty?" He grinned. "Besides perfectly browned bread, of course."

"Oh, I..." Again, she froze. The words froze. Jammed somewhere in her throat. There may have been a nervous hand flap. All the while those burnt-caramel eyes kept her pinned to the spot, watching, assessing, seeing too much. Leaving her nowhere to hide.

"You don't want to cook the eggs? Or...?" He hesitated, seemingly unsure whether to go on. "You are, I mean, you *can* cook eggs, right?" When she didn't respond, his forehead creased, his voice lowered, his tone gentled. "You didn't learn? Did no one teach you?"

It didn't help.

She shrugged; would not let the sudden wash of emotion overtake her. Would *not*. Waving a hand in the air, she swallowed deeply continuing with nonchalance. "No time." Or opportunity. Those bits were true. "I could have learned, I just..." She couldn't finish the sentence, scared the lie would catch in her throat and choke her.

"Ahhh... Don't tell me. Raised with servants or parents willing to wait on you hand and foot? The smart, focused kid in school? The career focused adult? How am I doing? Close?"

Not by a country mile.

She wouldn't meet his eyes, and yet she badly wanted to, wanted to see for herself if that flat-toned delivery was reflected there. If the disappointment she'd intuited was real or imagined. And if it was real? *Hilarious*. He was going to judge her for being a spoiled rich kid? The ultimate irony. If the lump in her throat wasn't threatening to cut off all air, she'd have laughed.

In her hand the phone pealed, and she snatched it up as the lifeline it was, instantly frowning when the caller identified herself. "Mrs. Danvers," Evie replied. "How nice to hear from you. Yes, yes, I'm here in Montana… Yes, Mia is fine and—"

The other woman cut off Evie's speech, wasting no time in getting to her point. JD's eyes never left hers and Evie wondered as she listened if her face was revealing first the panic, then her struggle over the meager options that were already lining up before her. Finally, she could get a word in, not a rebuttal or plea, simply something to signify the conversation's end. "Yes, I understand, thank you for calling."

All he did was lift his chin in question, and like she hadn't just been about to snap in two moments before the call, she dazedly slid onto a stool at the counter. "Mrs. Danvers is Mia's case worker. She was calling to check, and also to remind me of my responsibilities."

Her voice drifted low, and JD took a stool opposite, instinctively reaching out for her hand, his whole faced wreathed in concern. "And?"

Evie's gaze fell to their clasped hands, trying to ignore how good it felt to share with someone, how good *his* hands felt around hers, and too weak to pull away. "And," she continued on a sigh, "Mia must remain in my care, and my care only, until she can be safely handed to her father—and yes, sure I knew that. But—"

"Ahhh, got it…" Offering her hands a quick squeeze he pushed off the stool, grabbed two mugs, and headed for the coffee machine. As he made her a latte, remembering her preference from yesterday, he looked back over his shoulder. "You thought I would turn out to be the father, that I'd take your word for the fact, and you could get Mia settled and head back home?"

She twisted her hands, one finger picking at a loose tag hanging off an otherwise immaculate manicure. "It sounds callous to hear it put like that, but yes, I guess that's about it." She paused. "And the information did fit. You *are* JD Halligan, and what are the odds of finding more than one JD Halligan in Marietta, Montana? In my head it had to be you!"

"Funny thing, that. Those odds? They're actually higher than you think. In your favor."

"Meaning?"

"Meaning that you had a one in five chance of finding the right JD Halligan—well maybe four if you discount my sister Joanna Dawn Halligan." He squinted as he continued.

"And we'd all hope our father could be discounted as well." He shrugged. "And, that, as they say, leaves three. Me and my two brothers."

"Pardon? I—"

He held up a hand. "Don't bruise any brain cells over it. Just accept that my father and grandfather share a warped sense of humor and my mother—excuse the pun—humored them and went along. So, every kid in my family has the moniker, JD Halligan. I'm the eldest and therefore the only one who ended up using the initials as my name."

He was correct. It was brain-bruising stuff. Worse, it left a leaden pool deep in her gut. "*Three* of you?" As complications went. It was a doozy. Ditto for killing all rational thought. Both that and words completely failed her.

She sensed JD's eyes on her; sensed his curiosity, though his question, when it came, was from left field. "Evie, it's kind of bugging me why you were chosen to bring Mia to us. Are you representing child services? As a lawyer?" From her perspective it wasn't a simple question, but he lightened the moment with a sexy wink that despite her surprise, still managed to send things fluttering inside her. "Hey, I'm not complaining, but even so, surely there'd be someone with more—well, experience?"

The addendum to his question only made that fluttering more intense.

Still, it was a fair question. And the answer should have been shared yesterday. So, inhaling deeply, she took the coffee, warmed her hands around the mug, and shared the full story—mostly—glossing over the fact that she and Hope had been in foster care together. Telling herself it was a self-preservation decision; that it had nothing to do with not wanting to see pity shining back at her from those dark eyes.

As she finished, his whistle echoed through the silent house. "So, Hope? How's she doin'?"

Evie shrugged. "I'm not sure. I've been sending her texts, keeping her updated—well, only the things that wouldn't stress her until I know more. It's breast cancer and it's got a pretty rampant hold on her—I know that much." She placed the mug carefully on the granite. "I keep hanging onto the fact that there have been great results for women with breast cancer of late; I've read the stats—they're pretty good."

"I'm sensin' a *but* here…"

She blew out a long slow breath. "Yeah, I guess there is. Those stats are based on early detection, and Hope's wasn't. She may know more tomorrow and anyway, I just like to check in with her, tell her Mia is good. Great… Wonderful…"

"And she is," he said. "She's in great hands." Considering the original question, Evie knew he was trying to make her feel better and let it pass, unable to quite meet his eyes as he went on, "So, you just dropped everything to help out a friend you haven't seen in over twenty years?"

Evie shrugged off any implied benevolence. "She has no one else. It wasn't such a biggie… And, you know, we were pretty tight when we were kids. Anyone would have done it."

He watched her closely, so closely that she wanted to curl into herself to escape those eyes. As far as she was concerned, she'd told him all he needed to know.

Quiet once more descended. And stretched. A quiet like she'd never experienced in the city. Her mind still whirled as she chewed over their conversation, flicking out her tongue to moisten her now-dry lips as she did.

Thankfully he broke the silence before it became awkward. "I, ah, have some information that might help your search. My next brother down, Jack, paid a visit last night." He paused to shake his head. "Our friend the mouthy truck driver had stopped off in town." He let that settle, moving on when it was apparent she understood the implications. "I was talking to him again early this morning." Pausing he smiled.

Truly smiled.

And all her necessary body functions momentarily paused along with him. Wow. She hadn't seen his full-blown smile till now—but now she had—and dash it, now she would never be able to unsee it, or forget how it made her feel. *TROUBLE*. Uppercase. *Maybe she could kneel on that box. Stand on it?*

"I *meant* that I was talking to my brother, not the smart-mouthed driver." He laughed, his eyes crinkled, his generous mouth stretched wide over straight strong teeth. It was a heart-flittering sight, and she conceded yet another weapon had been aimed, one more she had no defenses against. Dazed, she tried to remember the conversation. Why had he laughed? She madly backtracked. Oh, JD, the brother, and the driver. Sounded like the beginning of a bad joke. Luckily, she'd caught up because the next bit was significant. "Thing is, Evie, he wasn't in San Francisco at the, ah, appropriate time."

"Ooohhhh." The moment called for the long *oh*. It was doing double duty. *Oh, that's what we were talking ab*out, and *oh, Jack wasn't in San Francisco*. Now up to speed, she summarized, mostly to prove she understood but also to negate any hint that she'd allowed herself to become distracted. By him. "So, you're saying that leaves us with option three?"

"Yup. My baby brother. Julian Duncan Halligan. Also known as Leo. Hell-raiser. Charmer. General pain in the behind, but okay guy."

"Wait." Evie sat straighter. "Hope mentioned a Leo… I recall now." Blinking, she let the rest of his words settle before leaning toward him, her gaze sharp. "But that aside, I just realized the actual significance of this conversation. Are you saying that you're really taking this seriously? That Julian—"

"Leo."

She frowned. "Leo?"

"From when he was a baby. Jack couldn't get his tongue around Julian—it came out Leo and stuck." He grinned. "I think Mom was secretly pleased."

"Okay, but you believe *Leo* might really be the father of Mia? That it's not some scam? Why? What changed from yesterday?"

"Full disclosure? It was her eye. It took me a little bit, but as soon as I saw that I knew the odds were against us for her *not* to be one of ours."

"The enlarged iris? It's not serious. I checked."

"Thing is, it's not actually an enlarged iris." He raised one hand as though asking her to hear him out. "Trust me, I've heard my mom explain it all my life. It's a rare birthmark that formed on the eyeball during gestation. And just so we're clear, the ophthalmologist who checked both my brothers claims he's only seen three in his life—my paternal grandmother, and my two brothers. I'm guessin' that in a few months' time, he'll be adding one more to that tally. My niece, Mia Halligan."

She watched him for a moment, letting those words roll around a bit. "You're claiming familial relationship due to her unusual eye?" When he nodded, she added. "I get that, especially if it's as rare as you claim. I also get that it makes my job easier and is basically what I came here to find—however, now, in the absence of the presumed father, that eye anomaly really isn't enough proof, and I couldn't in all conscience leave Mia until paternity has been verified."

"Do you mean… You're talking tests, again? DNA?"

"Yes, I think that's the only way to go." She paused to

choose her words. "Initially I was under the impression I was delivering a child to a man who knew something of this situation, enough to assume paternity—someone who could even fill in some gaps for me about all this. But now... This is very different. And while I really respect and admire your acceptance of Mia, I now realize this is a much more tenuous situation than I was led to believe—for everybody. So, yes, I'd prefer it if Leo took some tests."

His mouth pulled in at the edges. "Okay... So?"

"So, we need to get Leo here."

"Good plan—but not so straightforward, I'm afraid." He moved away from her; moved to the stovetop. "Eggs over easy?"

She nodded, heading to the toaster, working next to JD watching as moments later, a second pan sizzled, filling the entire space with the tantalizing aroma the way only bacon can.

Seated at the table a short while later, he reached to the platter in the center, snatching up a whole slice of toast before sinking his teeth into the buttery warmth. "Good toast. You're right. Most people couldn't have pulled that off so well."

Then the wink. Those eyes. And that teasing grin...

Yep. Trouble. *Big trouble.*

She waved her utensils. "You know *most* people would take more care when teasing a woman holding a knife." Biting back her own grin she basked in his laughter for a moment before pulling them both back to business. "So, Leo?" she prompted.

"He's on the rodeo circuit. It's his final year—or so he says. He's taken the big prize the last four years in a row. If you ask me, he's just showin' off now." He shrugged, but the action didn't negate the pride in his voice, nor the teasing. "He's worked hard. Mostly tries to make an appearance at Christmas or risk Mom's wrath, but the last couple of years we haven't seen much of him. I think Mom gave him a pass because he was working toward being home for good."

"So, you don't know where he is?"

"We can usually track him down through the rodeo schedule. Last we heard he was doing okay, but he's been hard to contact for the past month or so. That's not all that unusual, and we don't worry a whole heap. The rodeo crowd is like a family—they travel together, hang together, often bunk together. We've all still got buddies there—Dad, Jack, me—if something was wrong, we'd hear."

He may not have been concerned, but Evie's concern had grown as she'd listened. In her opinion, Leo Halligan didn't sound like he was ready to settle, and the big question hovered. "JD, if he's Mia's father, will he…? Would he…?"

"Accept his responsibilities? Of course. The old man'd kick his backside from here to Tallahassee if he didn't."

She pushed food around her plate, hating the anxious twist that was suddenly killing her appetite. "But that's not…" She swallowed the words. He seemed not to have heard her and for that she was glad. Her own childhood once more flashed through her mind. She'd have been so grateful for a safe place to live, for regular meals and a clean bed to sleep in. To be also loved and cherished would have made it perfect. That was what she wanted for Mia. Not just physical security, but emotional security as well.

Could Leo Halligan provide that? *Would he?*

They ate in relative silence. So much had been said, and yet still so much remained unknown and unsaid.

Toward the end of their meal, JD refilled their coffee mugs. "What do you think your next step will be?"

She shrugged. "Obviously we need to track down Leo—that's the priority. Do you think it'll take long? We're running out of time, so maybe I should be calling, as well. I have people I can get onto this."

Both his eyebrows shot skyward. "You think we're not trying? Or that you can do better? Trust me, I know my brother—he's way more likely to respond to us than a stranger." Pulling out his phone he scrolled to a number then pushed the phone her way. "But hey, go for it!"

She'd hit a nerve, and raised both hands, indicating surrender. "Okay... I didn't mean that... But you also have to understand that my time is very limited, and if Leo can't get back right away, plans have to be made. I can't just leave Mia here, and I have to be back at work in two days. That means unless we can get an indication of his travel arrangements today, then I need to start contacting agencies immediately.

I'll have to hit the ground running as soon as I return. My work is full on, and I'll need temporary help. At least until we can find Leo." Her hands tightened around the mug, concerned about the fact she was already dreading that moment. But what else could she do?

His shoulders relaxed, frustration obviously abated, his gaze suddenly more thoughtful. It was his mouth that caught her attention. Those full firm lips, now bunched; she looked away rather than stare, yet she so wanted to stare. "You know," he said, his voice dropping low, "you could stay. Stay here."

Something inside her coiled and tightened. "Stay?" The word hit the air on a whisper, and for the briefest moment their gazes held—right before both pulled away from the contact. And for the first time since she'd met him, JD Halligan appeared unsure of himself.

Making a big show of collecting plates he shrugged. "Yeah, you know. Just till we find Leo. Get Mia used to being here…"

His tone had changed. Now he was offhand, business-like. *Like he'd regretted the offer?* And yet his eyes kept darting to hers, and *they* seemed to be having a different conversation.

Confused, Evie offered a brief smile. "Thank you, but I can't. I can't take extended leave right now. I mean, I actually have a heap of owed leave, but it's a bad time, so ideal or not, I'll be headed home. I'll make arrangements today."

He stilled. Finally. "You'll at least stay until your flight? I mean, it doesn't make sense to pack up just to do it all over again in town."

That voice, low pitched as it was, juddered across her nerve ends. *Would she stay?* Of course she would, and she'd tell herself it was exactly for those reasons. Nodding her assent earned her a nod in return.

On cue, her charge made her presence felt, complaining loudly through the monitor at Evie's elbow. Thanking him for breakfast, and grateful for the interruption, she headed up, her emotions a churning muddle. What was it about that man that he could so easily upset her equilibrium?

Scolding herself for reacting, she forced her thoughts to the little cherub who was quickly and surely claiming a place in her heart.

Any reprieve, though, was short lived, and through no fault of Mia's. After changing the baby, Evie quickly glanced at her laptop noting at least another twenty emails—demands from the office—many marked URGENT. There was nothing abnormal in that, and she was used to it; used to dealing with crises and even simply queries from both colleagues and clients at all hours of the day and night, weekend or not. For the first time though, she felt the pressure.

She knew she had to deal with them, however, this time they'd have to wait and the pressure built. But there was no other way. She also had to feed Mia, watch over her, make arrangements, and wade her way through the multitude of decisions about Mia's future. Decisions that hung around her like a dead weight. And hating that she was already feeling dragged in two directions.

So much to consider. *Could she do this? Do it all? Be everything?* Doubt swelled, laced with a good shot of panic. Slowly lowering herself back onto the bed, her gaze naturally fell to the baby squirming in her arms. Those eyes, so trusting. That face, so like her mother's. Unsurprisingly an image of Hope flashed. So unwell, so frightened… And the answer to her quandary came, the answer her heart had known all along—*how could she not?*

Back downstairs JD was through cleaning the kitchen and Evie caught him just as he was collecting his hat off a peg near the glass door leading to the back terrace. She watched those muscles stretch and pull against the cotton of his pale blue shirt, the one that was such a perfect foil for that dark tanned skin. And her heart kicked in an extra beat, and then proceeded to throw in a couple more when he turned and their eyes locked.

Really? Enough, already… She wanted to sigh. No, she wanted to beat the granite countertop with her fists. Didn't she have enough to worry about? She'd only moments before been torturing herself with the litany of responsibilities she now had to juggle. *Really?* Did she have to add fighting the biggest lust attack she'd ever experienced?

Act cool! Pasting a smile her face, and holding Mia a little closer, she asked, "Going somewhere?"

He moved back across the room, and she tightened the smile so it wouldn't slip. She *needed* it not to slip, because if she was smiling she might not drool. *Oh Lordy.* This really wasn't fair. He even had a sexy walk, damn him.

❧

KITCHEN CHORES DONE JD had hovered like a kid near a freshly baked tray of cookies, watching for her, but he knew every minute wasted put the roundup further behind.

A message had come from Jack, a drama with one of the boundary fences. More than likely the fool had caused it himself, mightn't be too serious, but given the recent trouble he'd had with the foiled theft, he knew better than to discount Jack's concern, and he was going to have to go check on it.

Concern for his staff wasn't the only thing that had caused the twist in his gut though, it had been wound even tighter by the fact that he was going to have to leave Evie here, *on what might be*, her last day, and he cursed his brother every which way.

Now, back downstairs, she hadn't moved from her position beside the staircase and he tried not to stare at those long slender legs as he crossed to room toward her, instead sending a smile to the cute bundle in the lemon-colored onesie sitting in her arms. Mia's little legs kicked at the sight of him, and he reached out to gently tickle her tummy, his fingers tracing the journey of the fluffy bunny rabbits hopping all over the suit, smiling when she giggled and stretched out a hand to get him.

"Yeah, I have to shoot out for a while," he finally said, addressing Evie. "I just sent you a message." On cue the phone in her hand pinged. "Will you be okay if I take off for a bit?" He waved his own phone, quickly explaining his dilemma. He wasn't the sharpest when it came to picking up social signs, a point Samantha had regularly reminded him of, but even he knew this was about the worst time to have to leave. It wasn't merely the fact that her time here was so limited, there was also the other thing. The offer to stay. Not just for one more night, but until Leo returned.

He'd meant it, and even though there'd be a whole bunch of people who'd offer a list of reasons it might not be the best idea, in his head it still made sense. But even though he hadn't intended it, well, not consciously, they'd had a moment. A crazy, awkward moment. It had hung between them, heavy and sexy as hell.

It had shaken him and he had a fairly good idea it had shaken her as well. And so, despite Samantha's opinions, he *did* know this was a bad time to walk away. He needed to stay and smooth things over; get back to their earlier camaraderie.

And wondered who he was kidding. Evie Davis was everything he wanted and nothing that he should have; a walking temptation. One he had no intention of falling into—but hell's bells, that didn't mean he couldn't enjoy her company for the short time they'd be together.

Getting to know that precious little niece was going to be no hardship either. But instead, he was going to have to go and sort the mess down in the lower field.

"I'm real sorry Evie. I'll get back as soon as I can, but—" He shrugged. "I'm sorry it's happened this way. Usually there are people around—our housekeeper, Doreen, or sometimes our folks—but they're all away right now."

She waved him away. "We'll be fine. I have plenty to do—need to change my flight and get us packed."

His gut wrenched. "You're not leaving today?"

"No," she said softly. "I doubt we'd get a flight. I'm hoping for tomorrow though."

He nodded. "I'll be back." *Hopefully as soon as possible*, he silently added. He'd taken only two steps before turning back, capturing her gaze, watching her face pink up, seeing the added sparkle in her eyes. He wanted to ask her to wait up for him in case he was late. Told himself that it was because she was so tired and caring for a baby that he didn't. Instead, he reminded her of all the food in the fridge.

And called himself every kind of fool.

"*Most* people would know when backing off was the best option," he muttered as he walked away. And knew exactly how much trouble he was in when, even though he knew she hadn't heard him, he slowed, a grin forming as he half expected her return volley, and fought a swell of disappointment when it didn't come.

AFTER JD HAD left, it had been strange to find herself alone in this big house. Even more strange that it felt so empty; that *she* felt so empty. She lived alone in San Francisco—had for years. Being alone wasn't anything new, and yet this time the emptiness seemed to be not only in the surroundings but coming from inside herself as well. And the longer it went on the worse it felt.

There was so much she could do; *should* do. However, after booking her flight and getting Mia off for a nap, she couldn't settle. It was a feeling she was unused to, and so she rationalized it by telling herself she could take the opportunity to try to learn more about the Halligan family, to look around. Mostly just at the photographs displayed on tables and walls that had held her curiosity since she'd arrived.

One, a shot of several women at a picnic gave her pause, dragged back the memory of that lone woman on the side of the road, and she didn't know why. There was no one or nothing familiar in the photograph. However, moments later that memory was again obliterated when she was overcome with a poignant wistfulness—groupings of children in various poses, sometimes funny, sometimes sweet, but in all there'd been the sense that these children were cherished. She assumed they were pictures of JD and his siblings, but she didn't have to guess when she'd reached a wall display of photographs of rugged men caught mid action, riding bulls or roping cattle, hats held gleefully aloft. Evie wondered what these images said about their subjects. Chance takers? Bold? Carefree? And yet, she'd also sensed some reserve in JD.

Her eyes searched, honing in on their target. He was easy to identify, and her breath caught at the glimpse of rippled abs where his shirt had pulled free, of those shoulders, muscles straining.

She hadn't doubted it for a moment, but there was no denying JD Halligan was all man, tough and unyielding—and yet, she'd watched him with Mia. So gentle…

Was it possible JD was a man for all moments? She hadn't really thought such a man existed, but then again, she'd never met a Montana cowboy before, either.

Had Hope's experience been the same? Was that why she was so sure Leo would have stood by her? An idea flashed, one that sent her backtracking through the photos, beginning at childhood, identifying each child by age and then tracking forward until she was standing before a photograph of the man she was fairly certain was Leo Halligan. Within minutes a copy of that, accompanied by a message was winging its way to Hope, all those miles away. To the phone Evie had ensured she had so they could keep in touch. Her friend's response should clear any doubt, and perhaps if she hadn't been still operating under the cloud of shock at finding herself caring for a baby, she'd have considered it earlier.

There were probably a lot of things she'd missed and her lawyerly self bristled. Truth was that while she wasn't a stranger to broken sleep, the added weight of responsibility of caring for a helpless, vulnerable tiny human had turned her brain to jelly.

That admission didn't help her mood and moving away from the photos, she'd scoffed at the sudden feeling of loss, of something missing—that unsettling feeling that the house was even quieter than it had been when she'd first woken. But when on a scout of the rooms on the first floor she found his study, she couldn't deny that the house really did feel different without JD in it, filling it. She'd lingered by the door, not comfortable about stepping into his private space, noting the mess of papers cluttering the desk, inhaling what she'd remembered as something she might have fancifully termed as the essence of him.

Inwardly she sneered again at such absurd thoughts, drawing on all her inner strength for a return to rationality. It might have even worked if the phone hadn't rung at that moment. His voice kicked in, inviting the caller to leave a message. It was the same message she'd heard on her countless calls to him earlier in the week, and yet now, able to visualize the man behind the voice, it sounded so very different.

Caught up in that moment, she'd almost missed the caller's message. And then wished she had. Female. Young. Breathy. Perhaps she was offering to cook for him but Evie wasn't sure. She was in no doubt though, that whatever *Barbie* was offering was sure to be hot and tasty. Probably spicy.

And for no explicable reason Evie stomped back upstairs to focus on the work that had building up at a disturbingly rapid rate.

Concentration hadn't come easily but she'd persevered, and the long afternoon ultimately passed in a haze of work and caring for the baby. It shouldn't have felt lonely. It did and by dinner time with still no sign of JD, she was again calling herself all kinds of a fool for allowing the man to take up so much of her head space.

As the shadows lengthened, she found the food he'd offered, surprised that the fridge was so well stocked, and that at least eased some of her awkwardness at accepting his hospitality. Food didn't ease her restlessness though, and eventually, with Mia soundly sleeping, and night having long closed in, she crawled into her own big bed, trying to ignore the roaring silence surrounding her.

Rest did finally find her, after a fashion, but again it was a troubled night spent dreaming about her elusive host.

And damning both he and Barbie to someplace even hotter than the promised meal.

Hating that her thoughts kept returning to JD, hating that she had one ear open, worrying that she hadn't heard him. And she hadn't. Because by the time she'd finally drifted off, JD hadn't returned.

However, the two-word response from Hope that arrived well after the sandman had packed it in for the night, had cleared one doubt. *"That's him."*

Julian—a.k.a. Leo—Halligan.

Was that proof of paternity though? And did it mean Leo would accept his responsibility? The thought came unbidden and for the first time ever she questioned her choice of profession. Sometimes she just made life harder for herself.

Chapter Five

Their flight was at three, and being used to waking early, Evie had packed by the time she and Mia appeared the next morning. Packed and dressed for the flight—wishing it had been the pink pants. Instead, thanks to smooshed fruit that refused to be sponged out, it was the short gray skirt and the pink jacket, not the most practical for traveling with a baby.

The packing should have been a straightforward chore, but it had been beleaguered by all the conflicting emotions that dragged at her, and too many times she'd found herself lost in a daze and had to force her mind back to the task.

She'd rationalized that there were a load of reasons, first and foremost being that the trip had backfired; that returning home with Mia presented a whole swag of problems for which she hadn't yet found solutions, and needed time to organize. Of course, she also couldn't deny the pure joy she felt as being able to spend more time with this little poppet. But then there was the other one, the one she danced around and tried, without success, to ignore. JD Halligan.

Just like she couldn't ignore him this morning. Bracing

herself meant she was prepared for her insides to all but combust at the first sight of him. However, being prepared wasn't enough, and for a moment she allowed herself to stop fighting it, to savor the warm tingles flooding her body. For perhaps the last time. She could justify that.

His eyes tripped over her, burning a trail, making her all too aware of her outfit—and for few seconds, their eyes held. And held...

It was Mia who broke the moment, and Evie almost sagged with relief, released from his spell, allowing her to move. He'd moved as well, and her heart swelled a little at the interaction between this man and the babe who was, presumably, his niece. And surely that was what this was all about? Mia's joy was totally contagious as JD bobbed in and out of sight in their game of peekaboo while Evie one-handedly warmed the bottle of formula.

Only the baby's hunger won out over the game, but as soon as she'd finished, her eyes found him again. And once more JD's deep rumbling laughter mingled with Mia's sweet giggles.

While Mia fed, Evie and JD had discussed her travel plans as he threw together food for them. For someone who didn't have much time to spare, she'd expected to see more relief that she was leaving, and yet he'd seemed as flat as—as she was? That was crazy...

Attention was focused on the baby as they ate, their conversation polite yet distant. Later when it was safe to put Mia down on the floor, Evie found herself shoulder to shoulder with him, both leaning on the counter, mesmerized by the tiny human, who was doing nothing more than what tiny humans did.

JD's voice, not much more than a reverent whisper, reached out to her. "How do they do that? How do they capture everybody's attention like that?"

Evie shrugged. "I guess it's their superpower."

His chuckle came with a slight shoulder nudge, and she sensed a question was following. However, it wasn't fear of the question that prompted her sudden shift away from him to take a seat closer to Mia, it was that nudge; his body rubbing against hers. Even if it had been an innocent action.

Or maybe it was fear. Fear of what she might do back—like lean back into him and stay there. Afraid of what her eyes might reveal if she dared look up to meet the gaze she knew had followed her.

It would have been easy to claim a need to do something upstairs, scoop up Mia and run, and heaven knew, she wanted to run, but the thing about babies was that they didn't allow you to hide out forever. Aside from that, wasn't her purpose here to foster this relationship between niece and uncle?

Not that it needed much help and it was becoming more and more evident that not only would JD be a great uncle, he'd be a wonderful father. That thought released a flood of unexpected envy, which in turn prompted a flood of heat when that thought naturally led to the actual creation of those children and—

Enough! What was she doing? Where was her head? This was insane!

She needed action, to focus on something else, and when she detected a slight change in Mia's tone, she grabbed the opportunity with maybe more gusto than was warranted.

His eyes were on her as she prepared Mia's snack, making her more clumsy than usual, but after the third spill and her subsequent irritated sighs, he moved to the other side of the kitchen, once more leaning lazily against the counter.

Relief washed over her, but her slowed deliberate movements also allowed entry to more thoughts. This would be the last meal she'd prepare here for Mia. They'd have to get on the road within the hour. As she worked, Evie found herself reflecting on how different it would be once she returned to her city apartment—how quiet.

Her head immediately flashed images of JD playing with Mia, feeding her. And her heart filled.

That was quickly superimposed by images of those dark, burnt-caramel eyes that expressed so much; saw so much, spearing her, holding her captive. And her heart pounded…

But as she looked up and found his gaze still on her, steady and curious, it wasn't the expected surge of need that washed through her, but something more akin to loss. JD Halligan took up a lot of space, both physically and figuratively, and despite barely knowing the man, returning home suddenly had less appeal and all because... Because he wouldn't be there? Impossible, surely?

Thoughts piled in on top of each other. As a child, loss was the one feeling she'd had most experience with, had learned how to negotiate. Now, as an adult it should be easier—but it wasn't. This was different. This raw emptiness churned through her, squeezed at her chest, threatened to take hold.

It took that one perceived threat for Evie to straighten, pull herself together. She accepted pity from no one, least of all herself.

Giving the bowl of strained fruit a final determined swish, she turned, collected Mia and headed for the table. She'd barely made it when her phone once more pealed, and it took only the briefest glance at the caller for her to turn to him. "It's Hope."

He didn't hesitate. In two strides JD was beside her, gently lifting the baby from Evie's arms before turning to lower himself onto a chair—smiling, in spite of her mood—when Mia immediately grumbled, her reaching fingers letting them both know she knew what was in that bowl and wanted some. *Maybe Mia would be a food connoisseur? A chef?*

Albeit now a trifle forced, the smile was still determinedly on Evie's lips when she opened the conversation with her old friend. From the first words it was evident Hope was struggling. "Hey, how's my baby girl?"

Evie closed her eyes as the voice washed over her, weak,

raspy, breathless—her heart breaking at the images it triggered. "She's great. Such a little trooper, but I'm sure she's missing her mama."

A choking sound on the other end gurgled in Evie's ear and she straightened, stilled… "Hope?"

"I'm here. J… just a bit…"

"Maybe this isn't a great time. Maybe you should—"

"No, I have things I need to say."

Evie wasn't sure whether to be excited or fearful. "Okay… Do you have news? The treatment… Is it going well?"

"It's…it's ongoing. For now…"

Evie shook her head, annoyed for not making this a video call, because at that moment she felt an overwhelming need to see Hope's face; to gauge what that last comment meant. Before she could question it, Hope continued.

"I n-need you to do something. Several th-things."

"Anything, Hope." Any wariness Evie felt was overridden by concern. "What do you need?"

Hope's laugh was a poor facsimile of the one Evie remembered from their childhood, one that even then she hadn't heard all that often. "Perhaps you sh-should wait until you've heard me out. I-I'll start with the easy ones. Tell me about them. The house…"

Evie had been trying to keep Hope updated with messages, aware that the long gaps between Hope's responses were directly related to the treatment and subsequent consequences. Listening to her friend struggle now though, transmitted a whole other message, and Evie had to clear her throat to hide the little sob that had escaped. Instinctively knowing that what Hope needed right then was reassurance.

Evie moved away, out of JD's earshot. "Oh Hope, the ranch house is everything you and I dreamed about as kids. Spacious and created for a family. It's a true home, and oozes love somehow. It's in the little things like ottomans that are bent out of shape from years of supporting weary feet, or kids that have climbed all over them. Whole walls devoted to family photos, generations of Halligans. And Hope? They all look so happy." Evie took a breath, her mind reeling. "Let me see, oh and open fireplaces to curl up in front of… A big wrap around porch—and swings! Remember how we longed for that? And another tire swing hanging from a big ol' tree outside. And animals! We haven't seen them yet, but they're here."

"And my baby will have all that?" Hope paused, and when she began speaking again, Evie felt her tension release when it was evident she wouldn't have to answer that question. "I-I'm so h-happy. And Leo's brother?"

"JD?" What could she say? A whole load of words instantly began flying through her brain, but not any that would give Hope any comfort. Perhaps they'd make her smile. Or blush. But Evie was sure they weren't what Hope was expecting to hear. "Well, if Leo is anything like his big brother then I think Mia has won the jackpot. Though I think JD's ego is healthy enough without needing to know I said that." Her mouth stretched into a grimace. Had she said too much? Hope seemed not to notice so she continued. "He works hard. Loves his family. Respectful." She wanted to add—and adorably cheeky and a tease, and how his eyes crinkled when he laughed, and how easily he laughed, and that those eyes made her weak. Instead she said, "He's great with her and they already have a relationship. Her little face lights up when she sees him."

"So, he's—?"

Evie flicked a glance back at the man playing another game of peekaboo with his baby niece, using her bib for cover. "Uh-huh… Yeah… I think he's okay. My loser radar isn't picking up any bad vibes. None."

The sigh Evie heard held even more exhaustion than her voice had indicated at the beginning of this short conversation. "Hope, maybe we should talk again later—"

"No time. Please. W-wait. Let me say this. I-I got your message. About coming home." Hope paused and the gurgling noise again filled the silence, "Don't. I w-want you to stay until Leo… Please? Important for Mia to get settled."

"But I can bring her to you. Let you hold her."

"No. I don—I can't." Hope's sob drowned out all else, and Evie found herself clutching the phone tighter, not even trying to stem the tears now falling down her own face. "Please, get my baby settled with her daddy and her new family. Evie, please."

Stay? "But—"

"And s-send me photos. L-lots of photos. Ple—"

"Um… I mean, yes, sure." Evie closed her eyes, her head not believing what her mouth was promising—her heart pounding as she tried not to dwell on the difficult phone conversations ahead of her. Tried not to dwell on what the outcome of that might mean.

Yet, knowing deep down that whatever she was about to sacrifice was nothing compared to what may lay ahead of Hope, what Hope was about to sacrifice, and her heart twisted even more painfully.

A moment later they'd disconnected. Hope's voice had faded, and Evie heard another voice, a calming voice. A nurse there with her? And despite her own inner turmoil Evie was at least gladdened by the fact that Hope wasn't alone.

Whereas, she, selfishly suddenly felt very alone.

Evie slowly turned to face her host. "I um… I—" She drew in air. "It seems I won't be leaving today after all. Can you give me a minute to cancel my flight?"

❦

WHEN SHE RETURNED, in some ways, the new question in his eyes was the last thing Evie needed, yet impossible to ignore. That gaze, so steady and so still… Who was this man? How did he do that? Capture her with nothing more than his eyes, and yet embody her with the sensation that she was ensnared; had nowhere to hide.

And she badly wanted to hide. Needed to stop and think. Breathe.

And stop being ridiculous. Just moments before she'd been dragging her feet about having to return home? Now?

Then again, was the real fear of losing everything she'd worked for really ridiculous?

Heart pounding, she forced her gaze away from his, and looked down into Mia's little peach-smeared face, at that solemn stare. And if possible, the bands pressing in on her with so much force, squeezed in a little tighter.

Trust.

She'd seen that look so many times. Perhaps once it had been in the mirror, but if that was the case, she couldn't remember. No, it had been in the faces of the younger children she'd sometimes been in care alongside. The ones who'd looked up to the bigger children, or foster parents, with trust and hope shining from their eyes, both of which eventually dimmed until they—those lights—disappeared.

Breathe.

For the briefest moment she regretted agreeing to this whole thing. *Just for the teeniest, briefest moment...* Right before shame swamped her. Hope had already been dealt so many bad hands in life—to be faced with another, the very one she'd fear the most, was the cruelest blow. Handing her precious baby over into the care of others must be tearing her in two, facing the very real possibility of not being here to see that child grow? Keep her safe? Unfathomably cruel. The ultimate devastation. Viewed in that light, Evie should be honored to be the one Hope had put her trust in—and despite her own fears, she was.

Moreover, Evie wasn't a helpless child anymore; she was the adult who could maybe make it better—and Hope was trusting her to do that.

Inwardly she scoffed at her own self-righteous naiveté. So often she'd told clients that no matter what, they always had a choice—and it was true there were two options in front of Evie. Now, however she knew that if she was to do the right thing, the moral thing, the humane thing—that really, there had only ever been one road open to her.

And she'd taken it. The route had been set the moment she'd taken Mia in her arms.

She'd stay; do what needed to be done. *Do the right thing. Do what both head and heart were now both urging.*

And hope that her bosses saw that; respected her for it...

Raising her head, she saw that JD's gaze had narrowed. Evie swallowed, pushed down the bitter taste of shame burning through her throat and chest. She owed him answers, her reasons for this change of plan. This was his home. For all intents and purposes, Mia was his niece. His family.

Those reasons were still echoing in her head. It wasn't stated, but Evie also heard what hadn't been asked. That if this wasn't a suitable place for Mia, then Evie would ensure the child wouldn't be alone.

The bands wound tighter.

Reaching for the little person uppermost in her thoughts—who responded by holding out her arms—Evie held her extra close. Closing her eyes, she brushed the gentlest kisses across the baby's head, silently promising that she'd do all in her power to ensure her a safe and happy life.

Only when she'd gathered herself could she begin to recount the conversation, or at least offer the highlights. The promises—the photographs, the updates, the assurances. She paused, swallowed, her mouth suddenly so dry she thought she might choke. "Now that I'm extending my stay, I'll have to find accommodation. I, er, well, when I made the initial booking, I remember the manager of Bramble House mentioning that they were fully booked for the three weeks following my visit, so I can't stay there. Preferably I can find someplace close so I can come out here each day—get Mia used to being here, in case…"

"In case—?"

Evie felt a frown forming. Surely that was obvious? "In case she remains here."

His eyes had never left hers, narrowing as though in search of more; expecting more. When she remained silent, he sighed, ever so slightly bunching those impressive shoulders. "I don't make idle threats nor idle offers. I meant it when I said you should stay here at the ranch. It's the most sensible plan. Better than dragging the baby in and out of town. Safer, too. Roads can get tricky if the weather flips."

Their gazes held as Evie rolled over the offer. He was right; it was the most sensible plan, not only for Mia but for herself. It would save time, allow her more opportunities to keep up with her work. But… "I'm not sure. I mean…"

"Staying here made sense before—still does. Safer too. But I get it." He stood, took a few steps back, blew out a sigh and hitched both hands into the belt securing the jeans that hung low on his hips. Settling his weight against the counter probably would have made him look at ease if that totally distracting mouth hadn't begun some weird calisthenics routine, twisting and pulling until more words managed to tumble forth. "Look hey, whether you stay or go is your call, but I just need to put it out there that, you know, you'll be safe here. That I won't…"

His words stalled and frowning, Evie filled in the blanks. *"Murder me in my sleep?"*

Tilting his head back, he looked down on her through half-closed lids for what seemed like forever. "Oh yeah…That too." Then he winked.

Winked!

And her stomach clenched in response. She tightened her hold on Mia, feeling like she suddenly needed something to anchor her. Anchor the rest of her organs. "Oh… Um… Thanks."

❦

THANKS? THANK YOU? Thank you for not ravaging me in my

sleep? The words had hurled themselves around Evie's head as she'd rushed off, ostensibly, to make arrangements. Of all the things she could have said, *should* have said, she'd inanely and pitifully *thanked* him? How dare he even mention it! What kind of man thought that it should even *be* mentioned? Surely enlightened social standards decreed that *not* being ravaged in one's sleep should be a basic expectation? Not an *option* for him to assure her he wasn't going to choose!

Flushed and barely coherent she'd babbled her intent, her need to make a call to the office, turned and headed for the porch, desperate to get distance between them. Yet, now, sitting awkwardly on the top step in a too-tight, too-short skirt, too-high heels, and with a squirming baby on her lap, Evie realized that the end of the world wouldn't be far enough away from JD Halligan. Because even here, not confronted by him, that face and those eyes were right with her. In her head. On her. Consuming her.

Mocking her.

He wasn't the only one. Reaching up, Mia's fingers lightly patted Evie's cheek, grabbed at her lip, frowning as she babbled something in baby lingo. Grasping the little hand, Evie lightly pulled it away from her face, rocking it back and forth. "What? You have an opinion too?"

The tot did, her gibbers and squeals quite vocal before pulling Evie's fist down to her own mouth, gumming it furiously only to release it almost immediately on a frustrated howl that ceased the moment Evie produced a teething toy from her pocket.

Feeling slightly calmer, Evie watched, both sympathy and empathy flowing from her to the child. Sympathy for the pain and irritation the teething was causing, and empathy for the baby's obvious frustration.

Exhaling, Evie pulled Mia in close and stared out at the view before her. The neatly fenced corrals, the long winding drive, the sprawling red maple whose leaves were just beginning to turn, the double swing seat under it that would be protected from the summer heat by those heaving branches... All backdropped by the majestic aspens, by the jagged mountains in the distance, their blue-mauve aura, the snow-capped peaks so pure against that brilliant blue sky.

Such beauty. All at odds with how she'd just been feeling.

Resting her chin on Mia's head, she tried to analyze her absurd reaction to JD's insinuation, hating that the very thought brought a replay of the heat that had coursed through her. She closed her eyes. Was she really angry with JD for a breach of social expectations?

Or was she angry at herself for reacting to the image that had suddenly flared when he'd finally responded? Angry because the insinuation was too close to the dreams and fantasies that had plagued her the night before, and the one before that? He hadn't even said the words for crying out loud! And yet she'd imagined...

Imagined the two of them, her and JD, naked, entwined in a tangle of white linen bedclothes, tumbling around on a bed that had been passed down through generations, a bed very similar to the one in the room she'd slept in last night.

Imagined herself being ravaged? No, no, no.

Like a flashfire, heat started building again, spreading to all her most sensitive parts. Because, there it was again. The same image…

And there she was. Reacting in the same pitiful way. Heart racing, her body softening, heat rolling in like lava, demolishing all her defenses in its wake.

Oh Lord. What was wrong with her? It was like this place of her childhood dreams had wound a spell about her. Played with her head. It couldn't be JD Halligan! It simply couldn't—She barely knew him! *Didn't* know him! She had to clamp it all down. Control this absurdity. Find a way for release from these ridiculous fantasies. Help…

"Need some help?"

And there it was…

She almost choked. That voice… For a moment she'd thought that, too, was in her head. Deep, rumbly, newly familiar and straight out of those inappropriate fantasies. She wanted to laugh hysterically. Instead, she looked up, let herself drink him in for one long moment.

Yeah?

Bad idea.

Sighing was almost becoming a second language between

them and she waited for the words that would follow. "Hey, look," he began, "I get that this is all awkward and everything, but clumsy as I am, I was just trying to ease the situation. So, I've come to see what I can do to help."

"Thank you, but I'm—" *What?* Fine? Clear-headed? Calm? No to all of the above.

He waited; she closed her eyes, hoping the answer was hidden somewhere and she'd find it if she focused. "Actually, I'm not completely sure." She paused for a second. "Confused, I guess. Torn… Worried." There. She'd gone with the bald truth. Well, part of it. She hadn't elaborated. He'd nodded sagely through her response but she couldn't help but wonder what he would have done if she'd added the rest. Like, *and by the way, I'm also swirling in a sensuously laden pit of hot, sticky lust and the only way out is to tear every scrap of clothing from your body and—*

"Evie?"

Blinking she turned to him.

"I meant it. The way I see it, we—well, *I*—am partly to blame for this mess you're in."

Yes, indeedy you are…

"And I really want to help. I'm kinda at a loss here—"

I'm pretty sure you'd pick it up real quick…

"…but if you tell me what you need—"

Oh stop… Please. Just stop.

That was the moment Evie realized she could cross her eyes. She'd never accomplished it before, and there was a distinct advantage. The focus kept her mouth shut, which on this occasion was a good thing. A very good thing. For her self-respect, anyway.

❧

REACHING TO TAKE the baby in his arms was beginning to feel way too familiar. Trying to ignore the ridiculous surge of what felt suspiciously like happiness when Mia's arms stretched out to him in return was way harder. At least there was one gorgeous female in the house he hadn't offended.

The other was looking like she'd been kicked by a steer and was wondering whether to kick it back.

He'd obviously crossed a line, and crossed it pretty bad—at least if the skittish way she'd managed to avoid any bodily contact with him as they'd passed the baby between them was anything to go by.

His intention had simply been to help her out; assuming that making the call to her office would be easier without a baby in her arms. On a silent groan, JD stepped down into the yard and headed for the swing seat under the tree. Far enough away to give her privacy to make the call, but close enough to keep an eye on her. Though why he felt that was necessary was beyond him. Still, he'd relied on his instincts all his adult life—before that, too, so it made sense to listen to them now.

Silas, one of their ancient farm dogs, wandered over to check out the action and after one wary perusal, Mia decided she was in love, squealing and wriggling in an attempt to get closer to the German shepherd who reciprocated by swiping the baby's toes with his big tongue. JD chuckled at the interaction, allowing the game to run its course, teasing the old dog when Silas was the first to declare uncle.

Still perched on JD's lap, Mia also wasn't slow in showing her frustration at the dog's surrender, but when JD began to gently rock the swing she was happily distracted. Her eyes had widened with the first sway, her little hand reaching for his shirt, and JD secured his hold on her, grinning when she, once more, squealed with delight as the swinging continued. The breeze fluffed her hair, the fresh air pinked her cheeks and again that sense of all being right in the world washed over him when the baby eventually rested her head against his chest and closed her eyes.

His booted foot kicked them back, maintaining the rocking rhythm, and his heartrate slowed. How long had it been since he'd taken a moment simply to be? Since Samantha? But had he, even back then? Had he stopped to really see what was happening? Enjoy it? He'd been caught up in the fantasy, believing the spin she'd put on everything, bought right into it. All lies... He hadn't told anybody what had really gone down. Maybe because he'd have to admit to everybody else—not just himself—how big a fool he'd been. He should have seen it. The never-ending whirl... His gut curled. All the promises. Promises that were rarely kept—all with seemingly valid, over-riding reasons.

Declarations that he was enough as he was.

Then the big one.

Ironic that he'd be raking all this up while he held a baby to his chest.

He scraped his free hand across his face. Dragging up all these memories was taking him back to a time and place he'd left way behind; had zero interest in returning to. Even so, he didn't have to look far to find the reason behind this sudden journey into the past. The cuss rolling around in his head remained there. A gorgeous, focused city woman was bound to do it every time. Short skirt and heels wouldn't help.

His eyes slid across to Evie, in her suit and heels. Her hair, all golden and soft, seeming to glisten where it was caught by the morning sunlight. Long strands, pulled free by Mia's probing fingers, framing a face fashioned to tempt the gods—let alone a mere human.

And man, he was all that—human, and a mere one at that. Just as his body had been reminding him since the moment she'd appeared in his yard looking…

Stop. Don't go there… Dragging in a steadying breath helped ease the sudden tightness in his chest—disabling whatever force was trying to jam it up into his throat. His head was the other thing to benefit, allowing him a moment of desperately needed clarity. Gorgeous temptress—yep. Right here under his own roof—yep. *So?*

Nope. Been there; done that, forfeited club membership.

JD forced his gaze away from Evie, and down to Mia,

but like she possessed some kind of magnetic pull over him, his eyes found their way straight back to the woman he was trying to distance his thoughts from.

The incomprehensible murmur that had drifted across to him for the past several minutes had faded away, and from what he could tell, she hadn't moved a muscle since she'd ended the call. Statue still, sitting on the edge of the porch, her phone now lying idle beside her. The same position yet, somehow not the same woman. Not straight-backed and decisive, but hunched forward, her arms encircling those bare legs. *Lost.* And his jaw clenched when he responded to that image in the very way he didn't want to—with concern; a need to comfort—telling himself it was a basic instinct, human to human. Nothing more.

She wasn't looking their way, instead focused on something in the far distance. Very far distance. All the way to San Francisco if his instincts were correct—and his jaw clenched again.

Frowning, he pushed out of the seat and wandered back to the house, slipping inside to lay Mia in the stroller he'd erected the night before, wheeling it in to the corridor so they'd hear her before returning to lower himself onto the step beside Evie. Careful to give her space; to give *himself* space.

As the silence between them grew, he hitched his head back, indicating the porch behind. "You know, my mother went to a lot of trouble, spent a whole heap of money, ensuring we could provide comfortable porch seating for most of Montana—just in case they all decided to visit here at one time. We're still waiting for that deluge, but at the moment all that seating seems to be vacant."

For a long minute he thought she hadn't heard, but finally she leaned back, stretching her arms behind to support herself. "I'm okay, but feel free to make yourself more comfortable."

He shrugged, attempting to stretch his legs into a less-cramped position. "I'm happy to keep you company, but if we're engaged in some kind of self-flagellation, should I know the reason? It's kind of a rule I have…"

Evie side-eyed him and even in that quick glance he saw the shadows there. "Been to a few self-flagellation parties, have you?"

"Only this one. Between you and me? Not a fan—but I guess there's still time for it to get better."

"Don't count on it."

"Well now you've spoiled my whole day."

Evie looked across at him again, disbelief etched into every feature, her response arriving on a huff—part incredulous laughter, part incredulity. "I've spoiled *your* day?"

He kept his expression solemn. "Yep. And unless you've got something to top it, I'm kind of in the lead here."

"*Top it? In the lead? Are you six years old?*"

"It's a step up from three."

Twisting to fully face him, her eyes flashed all the fire,

hurt, and frustration mirrored in her tone. "Top it? Like having the case you've been waiting for your entire career to be snatched out of your grasp? Like losing your best chance at promotion in one fell swoop? Like being put on enforced leave, and your remaining case load distributed to juniors who've barely earned their right to the coffee machine? Sidelined without even a *how-are-you-doing? That* kind of topper?" Her hands slapped against her thighs. "And I haven't even started on how it felt to hear Hope struggling when we spoke."

She twisted back, but not fast enough to disguise or hide the tears that glittered in her eyes, welled, ready to spill.

For once he ignored his first instinct and didn't reach out to pull her close. Instead, he removed his hat, running his hands around the brim, glad to have something to occupy them. And hoped that by keeping it all light helped; that his other instincts were still working for him and not against him. "Yeah, okay. I'll give you that one."

Pushing forward, she wrapped her arms around her waist. "Big of you."

He'd expected more fire, but her words had been muttered, low, defeated. "You want to talk about it?" He'd deliberately kept his voice low to match hers, gentle.

The response was a while coming but eventually Evie shook her head. "Nothing more to say, really. Despite my unintended delivery, I believe I just painted a reasonably clear picture." She side-eyed him again. "Congratulations, by the way, your trick worked."

Turning, he tried to hold her gaze, his heart twisting at the pain still so evident in those gorgeous eyes. "Evie, I didn't—"

She shrugged, blowing out her response on a sigh. "It's okay. I get it. You may as well know what's going on. Nothing about this situation is normal—whatever that means. And like it or not, we're in this together—at least for the time being."

And right there was one big problem, because against all rational thought, he *did* like it.

Clearing his throat didn't clear away all the thoughts that went with that admission, but it did allow him to redirect their conversation, feeling a tiny bit cowardly for steering it away from Hope's circumstances, because even though he didn't know the woman, and really, neither did Evie, it was a heartbreaking situation, and a big one to unpack. "Okay, so, you've found yourself landed with some free time? What? A week? More?"

Her frown warned him it wasn't going to be an easy task. "As much as I want… *need*. And forgive me if I don't shout with joy."

"A lot of people would. Maybe you should try and make the most of it. Take some time to relax." He shrugged. "I'm only guessin', but something tells me you haven't done a whole load of that. Taken time for fun?"

"Fun? You're an expert on fun?"

Her sarcasm had been reasonably disguised by her light tone, but he hadn't missed it. He swallowed back a grin as he answered, "Fair enough. Maybe I am, and maybe I'm not. But I do know the first step would be to get you out of those clothes."

He was pushing to his feet as he'd tossed out the comment over his shoulder, not even bothering to hide the rumble of laughter bubbling in his chest. It was a fact that he, too, hadn't found much fun in his life of late, however, if catching Miss Evie Davis off guard could be termed *having fun*, then maybe he was better at it than he'd thought. From his end it was working out great.

CHAPTER SIX

ROOTED TO THE spot, she could only stare after him. "Wait. You didn't—"

"I did." Like the others, these words were also thrown back over his shoulder as he strode into the house. Words? They felt more like heat-filled missiles that speared her, each one somehow accurately finding its target.

What to do? She needed Mia awake, needed something to do, to occupy herself. Of course, he hadn't meant that comment literally. Well, probably he had, but not in the sense she'd initially comprehended. Heat flooded her face. *What did that even say about her?*

Hands shaking, she picked up her phone, and began shooting off unnecessary responses to emails that no longer needed her input, needing distractions to calm her before she followed him inside. Something, anything, to help her recalibrate.

She'd almost managed it by the time he again stood before her, a bundle of clothing in his arms. At a glance she saw jeans, and what appeared to be shirts, T-shirts, and sweaters. "I'm not sure about boots. There are some of Mom's as well as Joey's out there in the mud room for you to try."

"These are your mom's?" Somehow that just felt wrong.

His snort should have been answer enough. "Hardly. I figured my sister's stuff would be more your style. Stuff she didn't take to her own place. She won't mind. You're about the same size, maybe she's a little bit taller. Maybe you're a bit—" The words stopped short. His eyes, flicking briefly to her chest, silently, yet eloquently completed the sentence. He dumped the clothes in her arms, barely giving her time to catch them. And winked. And grinned. "I guess you'll figure it out."

It was that grin that saved him from her entitled indignation. Boyish, cheeky, slightly self-conscious, and kind of cute. Contagious. She knew his age from the brief dossier she'd received—only thirty-four. That grin had shaved years off that, and her own lips itched to grin back, but she held firm.

"Um, thank you. I think." It was true she was going to need more clothing than she'd packed. Specifically, more appropriate clothing, and it had been very thoughtful of JD to try to fill that need. A clean, lemony aroma drifted up from the pile on her arms, her fingers stroked the soft denim, probably worn-in to that perfect level of comfort. She hid the snort of irony that it wasn't the first time she'd been expected to wear someone else's hand-me-downs. Though she hadn't actually ever expected to do it again in her lifetime.

"Hey, if you don't want them…" He shrugged.

The words shamed her, reminded her that this was an extraordinary situation, that he'd been offering kindness, and she shook her head before raising it to once more meet his narrowed gaze. And this time, she thanked him with all the graciousness she should have found the first time around.

He nodded but the cheeky gleam had disappeared from his eyes, and inexplicably that saddened her, left her feeling alone and ungrateful. Hope soared when he suddenly spun back to her, hope that morphed into curiosity when she took in his expression. Confused wonder? Was that a thing? Must be if she was looking at it.

"Can't believe I forgot about this. Wanna come with me? I'd like to show you something."

No response was needed as she followed him upstairs, though her skirt and heels prevented her from keeping time with his long double-stair strides, reminding her how much easier it would be if she'd already been wearing something from this pile of clothing still in her arms. JD carried on up toward the third floor, but she took a quick detour to her room to drop off the load.

He'd waited at the top, in a corridor surprisingly well-lit thanks to the tall, wide uncovered windows set into the gables at each end. Perhaps sensing her curiosity as she followed him, he tossed back, "Jack and I used to have our rooms up here when we were kids. Leo was so jealous. Couldn't wait to turn eight—the magic age that Mom and Dad decreed made him old enough." He chuckled and she sensed a story there. "That was when we had our grandparents still living here, and before we added the full accommodation out the back for Doreen."

And so the childhood fantasy in her head continued to grow. "Doreen? The housekeeper, right?"

"Yup. Been here since I was a kid. She's away on vacation. More family than employee." He pushed open an end room whose slanted ceiling and part wall on one side followed the shape of the gable outside. Covered windows were built into both outside walls, and JD lost no time pulling back the drapes to reveal a whole lot of bulky, cloth-covered shapes.

Evie flicked him a curious look. "Tell me this isn't where you keep your long-departed relatives."

"Only the ones we weren't sure about." His dry tone matched hers. "To tell the truth," he said, now serious, "I clean forgot about this room. I guess Mom and Doreen are the only ones who ever come up here, now. No reason for the rest of us to venture up."

She moved to the nearest shape. "May I?" At his nod, she carefully peeled back a heavy white sheet, unable to contain her cry of delight when a perfectly preserved rocking horse appeared before her.

"Pretty cool, yeah?" He moved closer, and she sensed she could detect the fresh smell of the outdoors on his clothing, which was probably ridiculous. Did sunshine really have an aroma, or was this too, part of that long-ago fantasy? "I've lost count of how many generations this goes back," he continued. "At least four. My grandad played on it as a kid—and his dad as well." He ran a hand gently across the horse's smooth back, over that shiny nut-brown and white paintwork, and she couldn't stop herself reaching out to do the same, moving quickly to run her hands down the golden mane when their fingers accidentally brushed and they both momentarily stalled. Though his reason probably hadn't been the fizz that had zipped through her at the touch.

She swallowed deeply, forcing her head back to the moment. "Will Mia…?"

Evie noted that he appeared completely unaffected by their accidental touch which made her secretly annoyed with him, then secretly annoyed with herself for being annoyed at him when she didn't want him to be affected by her at all! Honestly, it all but made her eyes cross again. Thank goodness he couldn't read minds. Or could he?

His smile deepened, and she was sure she'd picked out a teasing gleam in his eyes, relieved when his response was merely an answer to the question she finally completed. "Will Mia ride this horse?"

"She sure will. I mean, that is…" He shrugged, seeming to straighten, his words carrying definite resolve. "She *will*. This will be her first horse—until she gets a pony."

It was the distraction she needed. "Mia will have a pony?" She felt like a parrot, repeating his words.

"Yup. We all got one when we turned four. Shetland ponies. Mine was named Candy Apple, and she was just as sweet."

Pushing their finger encounter aside, Evie's heart swelled as she listened, already mentally tallying up all she had to share with Hope, and perhaps there'd be more to tell after they'd uncovered more treasures. Like a kid at Christmas, well, actually, *like the kids she'd seen on television at Christmas*, Evie moved around the room, exclaiming over and over at the treasures within. A woven cane cradle, decades old and achingly beautiful, and now back in fashion which she knew from her hasty online shopping expedition before she'd left San Francisco.

A crib, a wooden high chair, perhaps not quite as comfortable as the deeply padded version she'd arrived with, but then again, also not handmade by a long-ago grandparent. And not possessing the intricate, lovingly carved animals that formed the legs and hand rails. Breathtaking work.

And more. A child's bed that matched the high chair. Boxes of toys, many handmade, all very used and loved. Then the most beautiful doll's house Evie had ever seen. Also a family treasure, handed down through generations, each room of the three stories filled with perfect, tiny furniture.

A lump formed low in Evie's throat and moved higher, tightening as it went, demanding all the space. Her eyes burned and threatened to spill, and she knew she should look away, distract herself, but she couldn't.

This *was* the fantasy—and Mia would live it. At least as

long as Leo was prepared to make room in his life and heart for this precious child who, like all children, deserved it all.

JD's voice broke the spell, and Evie fought to drag in air, to clear her head and push back all that emotion. "Every generation added to it," he said softly. "Dad added electrics for Joey, so all those teeny lights actually work."

Clearing her throat, she managed a smile. "Did you ever play with it?"

"Joey banned us after Leo, Jack, and I tried to shoot fire crackers out of the chimneys. Nearly worked too…"

Even with her heart still heavy with tangled emotions Evie could never explain, she managed a grin. It was hard not to, and hopefully a good disguise for all that inner turmoil. "You were one of those kids who had to play with matches?"

It was a simple question, softly asked; it should have prompted a simple response. But too late Evie realized that JD had picked up the throbbing undercurrent.

Her hands moved across the carved woodwork, slowly caressing. His hand reached out too. She watched, mesmerized as it moved closer to her own, ever-so-gently touching, stilling…

The air suddenly felt heavier, and she knew she wasn't the only one caught in this moment. Daring to look up she saw it in the darkening of his eyes as his gaze held hers—and her breath caught in her chest, squeezing gently as she waited for words that were slow to arrive. Words that came softly spoken. "Yeah, I suppose I've always been attracted to things that weren't good for me."

He was leaning in to her. Slowly, slowly… A promise in his eyes.

Her pulse soared, pounding loudly in her temple. She was suddenly lightheaded, unable to pull away from his gaze, those eyes dragging her ever closer.

Evie sucked in air. Opened her mouth to… What? Rebuff him? Welcome him? But the words that suddenly echoed around them weren't hers. Or his.

He was the first to blink, to draw back, and her face flamed. She wanted to run, hide, but somehow managed to direct a silent question his way. His response was a long, blown-out sigh. *Regret?* She wondered. His eyes once more held hers, and one hand reached out to capture a stray strand of hair and gently push it back behind her ear.

Then he straightened and turned toward the staircase, his voice loud in the small space. "Up here. We'll come down."

More embarrassed than angry, more confused than remorseful, Evie followed his clomped steps down to the first floor to find a strange woman in the corridor holding a dazed Mia who, if Evie was reading this correctly, was about to start to howl. Reaching to take Mia, Evie fought a whole new catalogue of emotions. Angry that an unknown woman had just cavalierly picked up the baby wasn't the only thing, fear for what might have happened, shame that she had left the baby unattended. A baby in *her* care.

Shame doubled down when the catalyst for her neglect, JD himself, turned to her and placed a warm hand on her shoulder. It was merely to begin the required formal introductions, but her traitorous body had a different interpretation and the fluttering down low she'd experienced such a short time ago once more began its insistent petal-soft dance.

Somehow, she managed a smile and nod for the jeans-clad, older woman, in the checkered shirt, Mrs. Francine Bouchet. However, it took only one more introduction for that fluttering to be cruelly doused. *Barbie* had entered the building. And she looked as perfect as her plastic namesake. But with long, long dark wavy hair. Hair that a man could wrap himself in. It took all Evie's self-control to resist an eye roll...

Painted-on jeans, peep-toe platform sandals, an off-the-shoulder green top that matched her eyes, and of course the requisite cowgirl hat, one with the sides rolled inward—and a covered dish in her hands containing something she'd obviously baked—completed the picture. She cooked too. She and JD would be very happy together.

Evie flicked him a quick glance. And paused. So, why was he looking so glum?

Barbie tottered off to the kitchen, obviously familiar with the layout of the house.

Her mother, however, kept her eyes trained on Evie and the baby. "Well, I heard the rumors but I have to say I plumb didn't believe them." The words were directed at JD but her eyes continued to be fixed on Evie. "And I simply had to come out and see for myself." Finally turning to him she said, "Well young man, it seems you've got yerself in somewhat of a fix, so it's a good thing you've got yerself answers near at hand. Now, my Barbie took quite a hand in helpin' raise her five younger siblings, so she knows her way around a baby. And a kitchen as well."

Turning to Evie she took no trouble to hide the head-to-toe perusal adding to JD, "And we all know how choosing a fancy business woman turned out last time, don't we? Didn't think you'd be fool enough to go and get yourself tangled with another one. Didn't I hear you'd once said that fancy city women and ranch life don't mix? Well, maybe you'd better remember that before you find yerself with more heartache."

JD had stilled, the tightening of his jaw being the one indication that maybe the woman had overstepped a line. She'd certainly lit Evie's curiosity. He opened his mouth, and she had feeling the older woman wasn't going to like what he had to say but then Barbie tottered back, a frown firmly in place.

"Oh Mama! Hush! You're being plain rude and in JD's own home as well." To her host she said, "Ignore her, JD, she can be a crotchety old crone at times. I'm sure you and Miss Davis are managing just fine and we should leave you to it."

So many things swirled in Evie's head. Admiration for

the other young woman; curiosity about JD's past then reassessing her opinion of Barbie's breathy delivery. It hadn't been for JD's benefit, that really *was* the way she spoke—and shame, once more, twisted uncomfortably.

Interested to see his reaction she glanced up to see him turning to her. The tightness had left his face, and in fact he almost looked like he was enjoying himself. Especially when he winked. *Winked*. Right at Evie. "We sure are, Barbie. Evie's a whizz in the kitchen too. Her browning techniques are a thing to behold."

Evie side-eyed him, hoping to convey her displeasure, which of course only delighted him and held until his attention turned back to Barbie. "You heard from Joey lately?"

Barbie's upward glance was as rapid as the speed with which she looked away. "She's… she's fine! Doing well. Surely she's been in touch?"

Curious at that reaction, Evie waited for JD's response, but he merely shrugged. "Sure, but I'm guessin' she tells her best friend more than she tells her brothers, right?"

Any response Barbie may have intended was ambushed by her mother who was obviously determined not to be silenced by her daughter. Evie didn't miss the relief that momentarily lit the younger woman's eyes, but beside her, eyes narrowed, Francine Boucher took another swipe at JD. "JD Halligan! That woman's not stayin' here with you all on your own, is she? What would your dear mother say?"

Beside her, Evie sensed JD stiffen once more, his wide-legged stance seeming to expand to position him closer to her, the hand once just resting on one shoulder, slipping right around her to grasp the other. "*Evie* is my guest and—"

"And it's none of your beeswax, Francine Boucher." Everybody turned to the newcomer standing right inside the door. Mid-sixties, flyaway blonde hair—evident even under her hat—jeans, boots, and a yellow sweater under a lightweight tan jacket.

And one of the kindest faces Evie had ever encountered. A face that was fixed on *her* and in particular his arm draped around her, before flicking to JD. Had one eyebrow risen ever so slightly? There was no time to wonder. "And as for what Catherine would say? Why, she'd hug him for displaying the manners he was raised with."

Francine Boucher barely batted an eyelid. "Says you, Nan Turner, but what about the rest of the people in town? Think his mama'd like what *they'll* be sayin'?"

Nan Turner strode deeper into the corridor, also carrying a covered dish. "And when has Catherine ever cared about what other people say? And as you well know, a rumor can only live for as long as people continue to feed it. We've all got that power, just as we've all got the power to shut it down. And as president of the town social committee, I know how hurt Catherine would be to know one of her friends abused that power."

Nan let that hang—*that* being an implied threat of some

kind. It obviously worked because Francine allowed herself to be guided to the door by Barbie, who was trying to hide a grin.

As she was about to step onto the porch, JD called out to her. "Hey Barbie, I'll mention to Clint that you dropped by. He's here working for me for a coupla days."

The brunette turned and her grin widened. And was that a blush forming? "You do that JD."

So that was how the land lay? And probably a bad thing that that knowledge arrived on a wave of relief.

"That's got rid of that ol' busybody." Nan's words penetrated Evie's confused ponderings, and she couldn't help but smile. They'd been the verbal equivalent of dusting one's hands together, and her satisfaction was evident.

Stepping forward, Nan formally introduced herself. "Well, aren't you the pretty one. Heard talk that you were a looker and they weren't wrong. Mind you, I shut people down when they started hypothesizing—and warned all those nervous mamas not to come running out here. Francine obviously missed my net."

Moving sideways, Nan then proceeded to throw her arms around JD, fanning kisses over his face as he bent to her smaller stature.

Keeping an arm around the newcomer, JD expanded on the introduction. "This one-woman cavalry is my mom's best friend. She, Mom, and Doreen are a pretty tight bunch. And don't let her looks deceive you—they can all get up to plenty of mischief."

Eyes glowing with what Evie perceived to be genuine love for her host, Nan moved back to Evie, this time her eyes drinking in the sight of the baby. Her eyebrows rose. "Definitely a Halligan. She's a little beauty, for sure. Oh, JD… Your parents are going to be beside themselves with joy." Her voice softened. "I'm not sure if you know, JD, that when your father had his heart attack, one of the things that saddened him at the time was the knowledge that if he hadn't survived, he'd have missed out on holding any grandchildren."

"I didn't know that…" The words were spoken so softly Evie barely heard them.

To Evie, Nan said, not unkindly, "But darlin', why did you wait so long to bring her forward? Surely, you'd know this family would never turn anybody away—especially one of their own."

Evie went to respond when JD interrupted and guided them all to the family room. "Come and I'll make some coffee. You might even need a splash of bourbon in it to hear out this story."

The older woman didn't argue when JD dumped cookies onto a plate, nor when cheese, crackers and cold cuts were equally unceremoniously dropped onto another platter—a perfectly adequate early lunch—and placed on the table before them. And blaming the mountain air, Evie, surprised herself by tucking into a meal she rarely acknowledged in her usual daily life.

They'd saved the story until they were seated, and several minutes later, Nan leaned back in her chair. "So, Leo, huh? There's been panic in town as all those starry-eyed gals and their anxious mamas try to work out which Halligan might be finally spoken for. You Halligan boys have been prizes they've all had their eyes on, but after a scare like that, there's bound to be a more concerted effort to snag you all—before it's too late." Her eyes flicked between Evie and JD. "Although maybe…" Her laughter filled the room, and when a wink was aimed in her direction from Nan, Evie tried not to frown in case she appeared rude, but in that laughter was something else. Like Nan held a secret that no one else knew.

As the woman's chuckles faded away, Nan became thoughtful again. "I can't say I'm surprised. This kind of sums up Leo. That boy has always thrown himself into everything he does. What's he got to say for himself?"

JD shrugged. "He's playing hide and seek with us. Only other time he's done that was when he borrowed dad's truck to get down to Laramie and smashed it up on the way home."

She pursed her lips. "You think something like that's happened this time?"

"Who knows? Last time he was just a kid and I had to get down there and haul his ass home. Hopefully he's man enough not to need that this time. Still, someone down there on the circuit knows what's going on. Jack's got the feeling he's being given the runaround, but he'll break one of them soon. Probably one of his old girlfriends," he added on a grin.

Nan chuckled and let that hang, immediately jumping back to Mia now sitting in her lap, and who had begun to grizzle as she gnawed once more on a teething toy. "JD, honey, would you mind going out to my car and collecting the box on the backseat?"

Alone with Evie, she smiled and reached out for her hand. "I can tell this has been something of an ordeal for you, hasn't it, sweetheart? May I ask how you're getting on with JD?"

Surprised, Evie shrugged. Blushed. "He's... he's been fine. Very hospitable."

For a long moment the older woman simply kept her eyes on Evie, as though she was reading everything going on in Evie's head. "Hmmmm, hospitable? I see..." She drew in air. "You know darlin', I met my husband Maurice and within two hours, I knew I'd spend my life with him. And I've never regretted one minute of those forty-one years."

Evie waited, but when no more came she smiled awkwardly. "That's so nice for you." And it was, but why...?

Nan's smile grew and she patted Evie's hand before releasing it. "I just thought you might like to know that things like that happen. And while they're not that common, they're also not unheard of. But when moments like that do happen in life, my advice is to grab them with both hands and run with them. Even if at first you have a few stumbling steps—the thing is not to let go."

Once more Nan's lovely smile was all aimed at Evie. "Honey, often those stumbling steps are due to things that keep us in the past. Now, take JD for example. Even big strong cowboys like him can find themselves tied up by things from the past they can't seem to find a way of freeing themselves from. But if someone wants something badly enough, they find a way. As long as they've got the right person to help them untie the knots."

With realization came another fiercer rush of fire, it flamed her face and Evie sat forward. "Oh, but JD and I aren't—"

She didn't get to finish because JD ambled back into the room, and still smiling, Nan turned to him. "Thank you, darlin'." The twinkle, however, had not left her eyes. "I was about to explain to Evie that as it happens, I'm married to one of the town pharmacists, and so I took it upon myself to pack a few things you might need. First of all, open it up, JD, and find that teething gel. It's a tube. I think this little missy will be mighty grateful for some of that rubbed onto those sore gums."

As JD rummaged in the box his head suddenly shot up, his wide-eyed gaze landing squarely on Evie, before he dissolved into a deep chuckle. Shaking his head, he didn't elaborate but Evie noted he chose not to make eye contact with her when Nan added innocently, too innocently, "And

Evie? Something for you too, darlin'."

Evie had no idea what had just transpired but somehow her body intuited a blush was in order. A response that seemed to absolutely thrill Nan Turner.

The older woman rose to leave shortly after, adding, "Now listen up. At any time at all you pair need a break, my arms and heart are always ready. I can think of nothing I'd rather do than have some cuddle time with little Mia Halligan. Lord knows once her grandmother arrives home, we'll all be hard pushed to get a turn, so I'd better grab a couple now."

They followed her out to the porch. Reaching her car she called, "Oh, did you finish off that steak casserole, JD? I've left pasta today and I'll come by with more food later." Her head popped back up to add, "But don't worry, I'll call first."

JD couldn't hold back the roar of laughter, and Evie suspected he'd been trying to hang onto it since he'd opened the box.

"Want to share the joke?"

"Sure you want to know?"

She sighed. "I'm a lawyer, there's not much I haven't heard."

His eyes flicked across to her, his chuckle already spilling into the words he was about to utter. "That little gift Nan left for you?" Again, the chuckle. "She left two actually. One was a giant box of condoms. The second, a tube of some cream that's supposed to enhance the experience. I figure you—or somebody else—rubs it onto your—"

"Okay, you can stop right there. I think I can figure the rest." She so wanted to be cool at that moment. Cool. Sophisticated. *But condoms? Clit cream? From a stranger. A stranger who thinks I'm having, or going to have, sex with another apparent stranger?*

Head held high she turned and headed for the house. "I need to feed Mia."

"We just fed her with Nan here."

"Change her."

"Did that."

She spun to face him. "*Most* people would be sensitive enough to see when the person with them is trying to suffer their humiliation in private."

"You're right. And I apologize. It's just that *most people* aren't any damn near as cute as you are when you get all flustered."

"Flustered? You call this flustered? I'd call it feeling murderous. And do you blame me? In what universe would it be acceptable to make a joke about you and I having sex?"

He sobered. "You're right again. There is nothing funny about the thought of you and me having sex. But darlin', much as I try to fight it, I can't deny that thought does make me smile. A lot. So?"

Closing her eyes, she dragged in air, hoping a dose of sanity arrived with it. If this was a romantic comedy movie, this would this be the time the heroine throws herself in to the hero's arms squealing *me too* and they rush off and have hot sweaty sex?

Possibly. Probably. But like all good romcoms they'd soon reach the black moment—that moment where they'd inevitably discover it had been a horrible mistake and they'd both be plunged into a vat of misery—at least until the soppy reunion scene.

Well, this wasn't a movie. It was real life. Better to cut and run. Much less stressful. Opening her eyes, she glared at him. "I'm going inside. I'm collecting Mia along the way. Then we're retiring to our room."

"But—"

She held up one hand. "No buts, ifs, or no-ways. Think of this as me saving you from that fated black moment. You'll thank me when you don't get plunged into the vat. Trust me."

And with that she turned and walked sedately into the house; his laughter ringing in her ears and her head full of images that she hoped to purge by focusing on all the work that awaited her; drowning herself in it.

It took till she and Mia were right up to their room before she remembered there was no work. Not now…

Botheration.

Her irritation lasted only until the full ramification of that clonked heavily into place. She rubbed her suddenly damp palms down over her thighs, and her head went into overdrive. What did all this mean? *No work constantly clamoring for her attention?* JD's words drifted back. Free time? When was the last time that had happened? *Had* it ever happened? Certainly not since high school. Setting Mia down, she stretched, seeming to try that notion on for size. *What did other people do?* She had no hobbies, no family, no one really close…

She'd worked hard to get ahead, to survive, to nail down that security she craved. Were they the only reasons? Or had she used work like a shield? Something to hide behind? Hope had been in awe of her *success*. But wasn't success about getting it right? Or doing something well, doing it better than others? Was that what she had?

Or did the world need to invent another word because right then, looking back at her empty life, *success* didn't sound like the right one to describe her situation.

And damn JD Halligan for seeing past the shield when she'd obviously spent her adult life keeping it firmly in place. That thought naturally brought the image of his face, and panic tightened its screws.

For there was the biggest problem of all. Without her work, where now would she hide from that man? From JD Halligan? Because surely, she needed to hide. Or risk—? Risk what? Her heart?

Was that even possible? But with that face still hovering front and center of her conscious mind she knew it was way more than possible. And so she'd have to be even extra vigilant.

And the devil on her shoulder whispered, *good luck with that.*

CHAPTER SEVEN

*P*LUNGED INTO A *vat*? Was that some legalese he wasn't aware of? Puzzled, JD watched Evie walk back into the house. Back straight, shoulders square. He noticed. And that wasn't all. He wanted to look away; tried to look away. But that skirt... The material hugged her gentle curves, curves that were accentuated with every determined step she took. Skimmed her slender tanned thighs. Did she know she had the cutest wiggle?

There wasn't a lot of Miss Evie Davis, but what there was seemed to be in perfect proportions. Contrarily, there was a lot *to* her. She was smart, determined, honorable, compassionate... He only had to look as far as her decision to take on her friend's problem to identify that last two. Loving? The way she looked at Mia, the genuine care and concern she showed?

He closed his eyes, needing, for his own sanity, to find some negatives. Then smiled as he thought of that mouth, that gorgeous mouth, pulled into its determined pout. Stubborn. Yes, Evie Davis could definitely be stubborn. And irritating. Sassy.

And none of those things did anything to negate the fact that she was the sexiest woman he'd met since—no, met. Period.

She did things to him, messed with his head. Made him forget she was everything he didn't want, didn't need. By nothing more than turning those incredible eyes on him, she turned it upside down; made him wonder, made him want...

Frustration burned. Maybe inviting her to stay had been a bad idea after all. Maybe everyone else was right, and he was wrong. Or maybe he'd been on his own for too long—and in which case it was even a worse idea for her to stay. His sigh hit the air on a cloud of exasperation. He needed to use up some energy; he was edgy, restless, off-kilter—and it had nothing to do with the fact that a little niece had entered his life. *That*, had been a shock, but a good shock. The feelings that had provoked were different—protective, caring, pride...

None of those responses had lit the fire raging within him. Those particular feelings were fully carnal and focused on one woman only. The one who'd just shimmied her way into his house. The one he'd just confessed to that she featured in his fantasies.

Yup. He was still that kid who played with matches. Even when, as a grown adult, he knew how much damage they could inflict if you weren't responsible around them. Like, if you lost your head, played too close to highly flammable objects—like Evie Davis.

This was ridiculous. He dragged a hand through his hair—definitely needed to do something. Hoping Evie and Mia were now upstairs, JD strode through the house, grabbed his hat and headed for the horse barn.

Raider whinnied as JD stumped closer to the black stallion's stall, but the plaintive sound didn't fool him. Raider had earned his name, always ready for action, and bad tempered to boot—but one of the most reliable horses JD had ever owned. The quarter horse's sure-footedness had allowed him to rescue calves and mamas from the most precarious mountain ledges and always navigated the steep inclines, culverts, and rocky outcrops without fear.

Reaching the animal, he stopped to speak softly to his old pal, running one hand over the satin softness of Raider's forehead, while patting his neck with the other.

Cody, hearing him, limped out of the feed room, a grin on his face. "Hey JD, didn't know whether to expect you down here or not." He tilted his head toward Raider. "He's been taken care of, exercised. I was just figuring we should put him back out to pasture seein' as you hadn't wandered down." There was the briefest pause before he added, "Been busy? Got a lot on your hands or so I hear."

There was no mistaking amusement in his tone, or the twinkle in his eye—and JD decreed there and then he might just do Jack some serious harm if his brother didn't learn to keep his trap shut. "No guesses about who you've been talking to, but if you don't mind, I'd rather stick to ranch business."

Cody West simply raised one eyebrow, but said no more. As both cousin and one of JD's closest friends, the man knew him better than most, and he'd pull back. Tall, and with shoulders that could heft a fully grown steer, he'd once been a rodeo champ, a hero to so many. To JD he was still a hero, having severely damaged his leg in an almost fatal bull-riding incident that happened when he was trying to save a fool kid, high on something, who'd somehow got in to the ring while Cody was in the midst of a serious tussle with Dynamite, one of the meanest bulls on the circuit. Deliberately throwing himself sideways, he'd drawn the bull's attention away from the kid. And suffered the consequences before the barrelmen could get to him.

Cody didn't need to work on the Lazy H; even at only a year or so older than JD, he could have comfortably retired for life, but he was the best horseman JD knew, and worked as the Lazy H's foreman because he wanted to.

JD pushed back his hat, watching Cody closely. "You're not on the ride?"

Cody's mouth narrowed. "Jack managed to get a few extras, even more than he told you. Didn't need me."

That was BS. They always needed Cody. "Your leg?"

"It's fine, JD. You taking out this fine animal or not?"

The words were delivered through a tightly clenched mouth which told JD all he needed to know, and he softened his tone. "Hey man, give yourself a break and get off it for a while. Pushing yourself isn't going to help."

"I said, I'm okay."

Their conversations about Cody's leg always ended like this, but it never stopped JD worrying. At times like this, when he was short-tempered, they all knew the pain was at an unbearable level.

Which was why JD was surprised when Cody's mood appeared to flip back so fast this time. "Besides, I gotta meet a lady later."

"Yeah?" JD's grin was absolutely genuine. Cody needed to get out and circulate again; meet people—female type people. And, yeah, JD saw the irony. "Where? Greys? Somewhere fancier?"

Cody frowned. "Not exactly. I'm meetin' her at *Java* so she can sign the rental agreement. She's taking the house on Court—short lease."

"You crazy fox!" JD slapped his friend on the shoulder. "You're using the rental on one of your properties to claim a date? Ha!"

Cody sobered. "Nah, nothing like that. She's just arrived in town, got a kid. I... kinda well, I let her have the keys before we signed." He held up a hand, probably to stave off any lecture. "There was something about her JD—skittish as a new foal." He shrugged. "Probably wasn't the best business deal I ever made, but she looked like she needed someone to cut her a break. Got the impression she wasn't keen on having me inside the house—nervous—so I suggested we meet for coffee this afternoon."

"Sometimes what our hearts say makes more sense than our heads. Proud of you, man."

Cody shrugged off the testimonial, turning immediately in response to a holler from outside the barn. "Better go see what Tyler wants. Talk later."

JD watched him limp away. Yup, the pain was bad today, but concern for Cody was no distraction for what else was going on inside his head. Left alone, JD stood with Raider, ignoring the horse's continual nudges, hints to get them moving.

But JD wasn't budging. The conversation had triggered something inside him. Someone else had been skittish a few times around him—hell—*more than a few*. Maybe for different reasons, but still…

After one hefty nudge that rocked his balance, JD looked back at Raider; cocked his head to the side. "You thinkin' what I'm thinkin'? Evie… She's probably only going to be here a few days, right? Can't take that long to get Leo to haul his ass home, can it? My head's tellin' me that I should be using every minute to get closer to little Mia. She's already had to suffer one upheaval, it'll be tough on her when Evie leaves."

The horse regarded him solemnly.

"Yeah, yeah, I'm hearin' you. More time with Mia means more time with Evie. And yeah, I know—my head's not the only part of my body that has a strong opinion when I'm around her. But hey, it's not like I'm some green kid trying to cope with his first inappropriate hard-on—and don't you give me that innocent look! Don't forget you had those church lady friends of mom's all-a-twitter when you displayed your full-blown feelings for Millie in the adjacent field. Whether she swished that pretty gray tail at you or not is no excuse."

Raider snickered, but JD wasn't going to let him argue his way out of that one. "But you're right. I cleared my whole workload so I could deal with this problem. Standing here yarning with you isn't doing that, nor is racing you all over the countryside." After sending off a quick text to Tyler with instructions for Raider, JD turned back to the horse, offered a two fingered salute and pulled his hat down low. "Good talk. You made some good points, buddy."

When Evie opened the guest room door a short while later, she was wary. It was right there in her eyes, in her set expression. But not as wary as he was suddenly feeling. He'd hoped the more casual clothing would make life easier for her, hoped it would even make life easier for *him*—those skimpy skirts and heels... Those jackets, buttoned low that invited people—*him*—to wonder what else hid beneath them. Jeans and shirts were standard attire around here. It would be easier.

So, he'd thought.

And he'd got that so wrong.

He'd forgotten his sister preferred her jeans to be skintight, claiming it allowed her ease of movement when doing the ranch chores. Like his sister, Evie was slight, and the jeans hugged her tight, caressed her...

The shirt? Orange and pink checkered. Tailored to follow her shape, and pulled tight across her chest. One strategically placed button threatened to pop, and relief swamped him when he detected something underneath it. A strappy thing?

Dragging his eyes away, he swallowed deeply, focused on the aged wallpaper. He should think about changing that out. Should think. Would think.

Dammit. Yep, he'd do that—when he *could* think—which definitely wasn't happening now. Especially with her standing in front of him looking like... Like *that*. Trouble was, he was beginning to realize that it didn't matter how she looked—all she had to do was stand in front of him and he'd still react. Worse, he *wanted* her to stand in front of him. Wanted to delight in every lightning change of expression, to hear her voice, to breathe in that pretty perfume that seemed to drift with her like a cloud. Wanted that, because having her in his thoughts and dreams wasn't enough.

But it had to be. If there was one thing life had taught him it was to learn from past experiences, and he was determined to do that. That meant he had to reel it all in because Miss Evie Davis wasn't the woman to risk his heart to, even if she did look like an angel and walk like a... *Don't go there*. He almost laughed. That warning should have come about three days ago.

Thankfully Mia broke the moment, suddenly having her say—a sweet burble of noise somewhere between a giggle and a shriek of laughter—bringing him back to reality with a thud. And a timely reminder. This was about Mia. Nothing else.

Pull it together. Be polite. Courteous. Responsible. Act like the thirty-four-year-old man he was, and not the sixteen-year-old hormone-driven teenager he'd reverted to since the moment he'd laid eyes on that woman.

He could do it.

Sure, he could.

❦

EVIE COULDN'T REMEMBER the last time she'd worn jeans, and there were all kinds of things wrong with that self-revelation. She also couldn't remember the last time—if ever—a man had flipped her emotions around like this man did. And there were all kinds of things wrong with that as well.

It undermined the very fabric of who she had molded herself to be. Constantly feeling out of control, like a leaf tossed around on an ocean wave, was terrifying for a person who prided herself on always being rational, in control. And yet with that fear came other feelings. Things she'd not really experienced. Things that felt good.

Like her heart doing a joyful rhumba when the man she

expressly did not want to see is suddenly standing right in front of her. Like that feeling of a lit-fuse-line sizzling a path through her entire body, following the path his eyes forged as they roved over her.

Yes, there were all kinds of things wrong there.

He cleared his throat and she recentered. Perhaps he did as well. "I, er—" That only made things worse. The nerve ends that the searing fuse had awakened, now raw and exposed, rejoiced as that gravelly voice stroked every single one as it passed over them.

Was there no hope for her? Evie somehow suppressed the huge sigh that was suddenly building within her. It seemed all roads led to the same place. Her body was definitely betraying her and showing no remorse. The heart that had been happy dancing moments before at least obliged with a slight downward swing, but somehow she knew it wouldn't last.

And proved herself to be completely correct when that traitorous heart soared again the moment he resumed speaking.

"I figure I owe you a proper apology. I was a horse's rear end earlier. I made light where I shouldn't have, however I was—" His lips clamped, his body shifting ever so subtly, somehow still managing to capture and hold her gaze with some kind of magnetic pull that breaking free of seemed almost impossible. Her chest tightened—held—then released when the intensity in his eyes suddenly dimmed leaving her to imagine he'd lost some inner battle. And contrarily yearning to discover the details of that battle even while telling herself it was for the best that she didn't know.

His voice reached out to her again, his gaze now on the baby behind her. "Ahhh, yeah—" A sigh. "Thinking about Mia; how to make her transition easier. And maybe I could help out with the photos and information for Hope. So, I was thinking maybe we could take Mia for a walk around the house yard. Wander down to the stables."

The feeling that he'd been going to say something different, more intimate, something about the two of them, lingered, but there was sincerity in his eyes. That *something* both intrigued her and terrified her all at once, but he was correct—this whole thing was about baby Mia. So, while words were still having difficulty making it past the boulder parked in her throat, she simply nodded, scooped up the baby and followed him downstairs.

Between them both they'd nearly managed to unpack all the baby paraphernalia Evie had organized to be delivered, so the baby pouch was easy to find. She was trying to fathom how to use it when JD surprised her by suggesting he put it on instead. Her indignant response flew all the way to the tip of her tongue before sanity prevailed. This had nothing to do with equality; rationally it made more sense for him to carry Mia, after all this was about the baby bonding with her family.

Even if it did seem like her bones were melting at the

sight of that tiny bundle cuddled in against that strong broad chest.

Her eyes drank in the sight, and kept right on drinking.

Of course, he caught her looking. Of course he did.

He also grinned. And Evie silently began reciting the alphabet backward. Was it possible to really yearn for someone, and yet be really irritated by them all at the same time?

She was glad he'd suggested she grab a coat, another loaner—the production of putting it on providing adequate reason to avoid making eye contact. And speech.

Outside she continued with the nonchalance.

However, the problem with nonchalance is that it's almost *always* feigned, and therefore, not always a reliable course of action—all of which was going through Evie's head as she found herself darting furtive little glances his way as they walked—and with interesting results.

JD was pretending nonchalance with her just as studiously as she with him! But like her, he'd given himself away when she'd caught his glance aimed her way.

It was a ludicrous situation and could end up with one or both of them walking into a pole! Or a barn! Or something else they didn't see while they were sneaking glances and pretending they weren't, instead of actually paying attention to where they were walking.

"One of us is going to walk into a pole."

He snorted, and she caught a quirked eyebrow. "A *pole*?

No poles."

She sighed. "A tree."

"Not on this pathway."

"Fall into a ditch."

"Nope. My eyes are front and center. No ditches." Another glance flicked her way. "Are you a fatalist by the way?"

The air had cooled and Evie pulled the coat tighter. "Fatalist? No, I mean why—"

"You mean, why are you predicting unlikely, hardly fatal, yet potentially harmful scenarios?" he finished for her. "I admit I'm mighty intrigued."

She shrugged. "I'm not—a fatalist that is." Yes, she was. "I mean, I was just being…cautious. After all, we are charged with the care of a very precious cargo." A sigh escaped. "And okay, I, um, well I didn't think we were paying enough attention."

"Uh huh… So this is about Mia? Not about—?"

Choosing to be obtuse was not always a bad thing. It was merely a choice—and she was choosing it now. "Um…family?"

"Ahhh… Family." He nodded. Patronizingly. *He* was obviously choosing smug. "Now that wasn't where I thought this was going at all. You see, I was kinda hung up on the *reason* you thought we might not have been paying attention."

"Still can't leave those matches alone," she muttered dryly before drawing in a steadying breath and declaring loudly,

"The view! That's the reason." She waved her hands to give credence to her response. And surely even he couldn't argue with that. It was stunning. Even in the growing gloom of the afternoon.

"You mean those magnificent trees that are providing us with a breathtaking color show only nature could provide? That wide Montana sky? So blue at times it hurts to look at it? Copper Mountain? Proud and mighty, straining high into the air, humblin' us with its beauty? You mean *that* view? *The one I see every day?*" His pause was underscored by a raised eyebrow. "Sweetheart, there's not much I love more than that view, but to distract me to the extent that I might do myself an injury?"

He hadn't had to respond with his tongue firmly in his cheek, it had been clearly implied in his tone. "Very poetic cowboy." The snip had been halfhearted and Evie blew out the air that had pooled in her chest, feeling her shoulders drop. "Okay, okay… I get it. I guess—" But it was no use, any further words failed her.

They'd reached a corral fence and he stopped, moving to stand in front of her, blocking her progress; rested his arm along the rail. His eyes seemed to rove over her face, the path as gentle as a caress. "It's okay," he began softly. "Evie—"

It was just one word; her name—or maybe the way he said it—and yet her chest tightened. Mouth suddenly dry she waited, hoping maybe to hear that what he'd said earlier about fantasizing about her had been true, and yet at the same time dreading that he might do exactly that. Her heart picked up speed and she wished she was the one holding Mia, wished she had something else to focus on, something to occupy her hands that were suddenly restless, wanting to reach out and—*what?*

Her heartbeat thundered in her ears and at first the only sign she had that something had broken the moment had been what she read on JD's face. Frustration in the small shake of his head, eyes that dimmed with regret and then seemed to close her out; turn away. Confused she followed the focus shift, the words she'd missed finally penetrating.

"Yo! Ma'am? Ma'am? That cowboy botherin' you in any way?"

It seemed neither she nor JD were destined to manage a full sentence that afternoon, but as her mind began to clear, her interest was piqued by the man hobbling toward them, a grin as wide as the Montana sky ensuring his words held no serious intent.

JD, however, shared none of the other man's levity, his groan long and low.

"Your brother?" Her words hit the air on a husky whoosh, the residue of what she'd just been feeling, and she hastened to cover it with a feigned cough. Had JD noticed?

Yes, he had—turning to her, holding her gaze for that moment too long, his own eyes narrowed—before turning back to the interloper, his scowl such a contrast to the other's teasing expression. "Yup. Jackson Dean Halligan. Known as

Jack. General pain in the a—" His eyes slipped back to Evie and he adjusted his hat, pulling it lower as he amended his comment. "Abdomen."

Evie smothered a grin, and turned to Mia. "Hey baby girl, another uncle. Look!" And surely no one but herself would have detected that slight quiver still in her voice.

However, it was she doing all the looking a second later when the man joined them. Such likeness! There was no way these boys would ever be able to deny a familial relationship. Just as tall and well built, and as devastatingly handsome as JD—yet Evie had a feeling Jackson Halligan didn't quite take life as seriously as his older brother.

JD addressed him first. "You heard from Leo?"

The other man's eyes flicked to Evie, and she felt her body still as she waited for the answer, wondering whether he'd had more luck than she'd had.

That answer began with a slight shake of his head, the words delivered quietly. "There's something goin' down. I'm still getting the runaround—but I'm chasin' it; messaged that I've got that DNA test organized for when he gets back."

JD's eyes narrowed. "Why aren't you out on the round-up?" His gaze slipped to range across his brother's lower half. "You hurt?"

Ignoring his brother, Jackson Halligan's expression lightened again, and instead of responding, he extended his hand toward Evie. "Excuse my brother. He's let life turn him into a miserable Grinch." His laughter carried the next words, both accompanied by a tip of the tan felt cowboy hat now bearing a dark line of sweat right above the brim. "Jack Halligan, ma'am. You must be Evie?" Releasing Evie's hand, he then turned to the baby in JD's arms. "And you must be baby Mia. Well, aren't you a little beauty." His eyes flicked across to his brother. "Two beautiful girls, eh bro? I can see why you were so anxious to get yourself out of that dusty old roundup."

If possible, JD's eyes narrowed even more. "What are you doing back so early, Jack?"

Another voice joined in to answer and Evie suddenly had the feeling of being enclosed by a wall of muscle. Three big hunky men. Were all Montana cowboys like this? Tall, built, and gorgeous? If news got out, there'd be a stampede of anxious women determined to stake a claim on one! Seriously.

Evie blamed her sudden lack of industrial endeavor for the reason her eyes suddenly darted across to find JD. Her thoughts were flirting with the impossible—and improbable… It had to be because her work had been taken from her and she was temporarily lost; restless. Had to be. She did not want to stake a claim. No. Just no.

The newcomer's words, aimed at JD, resettled her attention. "Jack took Trix out today." Having said that, he immediately turned toward Evie. "Cody West ma'am. Cousin to these two reprobates—and I help out around here, too. Real nice to meet you." To Mia he said, "Hey little one, you look mighty cozy there."

"Yeah, sure suits you, bro."

Interestingly JD's mood had suddenly lifted, and his gaze flicked to Cody before traveling back to his mouthy brother. In fact, JD's lips had begun to quiver. Watching on, Evie's breathing quickened. *Full, firm, quivering lips simply signal amusement, rendering all lustful reactions inappropriate.* She needed that on a wall. A daily mantra.

Oblivious to her inner turmoil, JD, eyes now alight, focused on his brother. "You took Trix? How did that go?"

Jack's big shoulders slumped. "Not good. Tyler and I have just been rubbing him down. I was on my way up to give you the bad news." Regret deepened his tone. "I thought he'd picked up a stone but I think he's turned his foot. He went lame on me and it was getting real bad so I've walked him home the last three or four miles. I told Cody we need to get him checked out."

"Lame, huh?" JD barely got the words out, hardly able to control his laughter. Cody was no better.

Jack bristled, pushing his hat further back on his head. "Not sure what's so amusing. It could mean you've lost a good quarter horse if his leg is as badly damaged as I think it is."

"Riiii-gh-t." JD drew out the word. "So, you examined him? Found the damaged area?"

Jack shrugged, and JD continued. "Serious, huh? Had to walk him home? Down the mountain? Over the rocks and rubble. Must have taken a while, hence your sore feet. Can't have been fun. Probably wrecked a good pair of boots... Shame." At Cody's discreet nod, JD turned slightly to a movement in the previously empty corral beside them, hefting a thumb in that direction. "Just so we're clear here though, we're talking about *that* Trix? That same horse?"

JD nudged Evie, silently indicating she should keep her eyes on his brother whose own eyes, naturally turned to the corral—and the reaction on Jack's face was priceless. Shocked surprise gave way to confusion that in turn gave way to full-blown exasperation. Because, there, obviously, was Trix, a glorious chestnut colored beast, matching mane flying as he happily frolicked around the enclosure. Whatever game he was playing called for his legs to pump up and down, his tail to swish and swing, and his head, with the pretty white markings down his nose, to bob cheekily. All in all, offering a joyfully spirited display. Very spirited. When the horse paused and looked across at his audience, the mischievous whinny was too much, and three of the four looking on dissolved into laughter, even Mia kicked her little legs and squealed. Jack, however, was still speechless.

JD finally regained some control, enough to address his brother. "You need to get out here to the ranch more often, bro. You're getting soft. I take it no one reminded you why he got his name? Trickster? That horse has got way too much personality and way too many smarts. Pretending to go lame is one of his party tricks; pulls it out whenever he gets a new rider—someone who isn't onto him and his mischief."

JD and Cody were still having too much fun at Jack's expense. However, when Jack's head rocked back, Evie sobered; tensed. Unused to the mechanics of typical sibling interaction, she'd begun to wonder if JD had gone too far, relieved to join in with the others when Jack's whoop of laughter—slow to come at first—rang out across the surrounding fields.

For several minutes after that she watched on through a whole lot of back-slapping and swapped jibes, watched the brothers and their cousin—obviously as comfortable with the Halligans as they were with each other—and her faith that Mia would be in safe hands solidified.

The child would learn to give and take, to laugh and support as well as take strength in the fact that she, too, would be supported. Because while these tough cowboys might not put it into exactly these words, Evie saw the love there under the teasing; love they so obviously shared. Saw them stop and fuss over little Mia, who lapped it up and rewarded them all with gummy smiles—and saw three big husky cowboys reduced to marshmallow as a result.

Her heart was full, and her eyes still wet from laughter when the group made to break up. Jack to go back to his place in Marietta township, and Cody also headed that way to meet with his new tenant.

Evie looked across at the man still standing in front of her, and as though somehow strangely connected by the same switch, they laughed. Laughter that wound down into smiles, real smiles that reached their eyes and came from their hearts; linked them as only a shared experience can do.

It was a moment. A connection. Evie had experienced so few in her life that it felt all the more special, and she wanted to hold it, even reluctant to breathe. She knew she had to, but held off as long as she could, scared that movement would somehow break the tie that kept them bound—knowing, yet studiously ignoring the truth—that the tie was tenuous. For this very small moment though, she simply let herself feel. This felt different. Good, different. This was real.

JD moved first. Tossing an arm around her shoulders, he guided her toward the horse barn. "Come on. Time to introduce the two prettiest ladies in Montana to a good friend of mine. He gave me some handy advice this afternoon."

Chapter Eight

JD had no idea what had happened but he wasn't fool enough to question it. And he couldn't think of any man alive who would if it meant they got to bask in the warmth of the smile Evie Davis had just showered upon him. He thought back to all the emotions he'd seen flash across that beautiful face over the past couple of days, and yet it kind of felt like he was seeing the real Evie for the first time—like a mask had slipped.

His arm felt good resting on her shoulders, and even better she hadn't flinched or pushed him away—though why that was *better* was still an anathema to him given all the arguments he'd put up for why getting closer to her would be a bad idea. But maybe today wasn't the day to question, just go with the flow.

Evie reached across to Mia, who grabbed onto one finger, and was quite excited to have captured it if the squeals and kicking legs were any indication. Evie's reaction wasn't quite as effusive, though JD quietly admitted that he'd like to have seen that, but her chuckle rippled through him, and that made him wonder about other things.

Like, what if this was his own family with him at that moment? If the woman beside him was his partner and Mia their child? If walking along with them, across the land he loved so much, cuddled up to each other, all three together, in the cooling air—like, if it was real—how would that make him feel?

The answer punched its way in, solid and powerful. It would make him feel—whole. Maybe he hadn't expected that response to arrive quite so forcefully, but he wasn't really surprised. He'd never denied this was what he ultimately wanted. A wife, a partner in life, one he loved more than he needed air, and one who loved him back just as mightily. Someone to grow old with, someone who'd still want to sit on a porch swing at the end of a long day and hold his hand when they were both wrinkled and gray. A family spawned as a result of that love who would live a life of both security and freedom—just as he had.

For a while a few years back, he'd thought he'd found that. But now he knew better; knew that looking in the wrong place would only bring heartache and disappointment.

Unfortunately, as much as the rest of him wanted to believe the woman under his arm might feel like that potential partner right then, ultimately, she was in the wrong place.

A fact that was even harder to swallow when she looked up at him with those incredible blue eyes, soft and full of questions. "You okay?"

Was he? He sure as hell didn't know. "Sure." Frowning he asked, "How about you? You okay? Feeling any better?" he ventured softly. "You know, about the job and everything?"

He felt her sigh, saw the confusion in her eyes as she turned to him. "My work? I don't know that I've fully even processed it yet. I reach for my laptop or phone, expecting to battle my way through a barrage of questions and demands, and they're just not *there*."

She sounded lost, and aside from pushing back an overwhelming need to try to make life right for her again, it prompted the obvious question. What kind of person is lost when their work is taken from them? *Somebody who lives to work.* "That could be a good thing, though, right? I mean, I know it's been a big thing for you to have to face, but maybe it could be a blessing? So, when you return you'd be refreshed; better able to tackle it all?"

She folded her arms across herself and he tucked her in closer to share his warmth. That was the thing about Montana weather; it could turn faster than you can say *grab a coat*. "I guess in theory it works that way."

"Look at this way. How long since your last vacation? Maybe you're ready for a break?"

She didn't immediately respond, and he sensed her frown before he peeked to check it out. It deepened when she caught his eye. "It's been a while…"

A while could mean a lot of things. Several months, a

year, a few weeks... But JD had a strong feeling she meant A While, both words capitalized. His mother was a great believer in fate, and maybe this case was a just argument for that. Maybe this situation was destined to happen because it was what Evie needed? Although, he figured it would take a hell of a lot more persuasion than he could muster to convince her of that, so he let it ride, instead squeezing her shoulder, offering reassurance. "Your work is important, huh?"

She nodded and his heart fell. Yup. Definitely not a girl prepared to settle down on a ranch and make babies. Not that he'd expect any woman to give up a career, but they weren't talking only about a career here, they were talking about a whole life, and something was telling him that Evie Davis wasn't ever going to change hers.

They'd reached the first horse barn and JD prepared himself for what was to come. This would settle his mind. He'd missed the clues with Samantha; thought it was cute, funny, at first how she curled her nose, made a big production of the smell—even though his barns were regularly mucked out, fresh straw laid twice a day. There wasn't much about ranch life that Samantha hadn't curled her nose up at, but he'd been too blinded by her to pick up the signs. Others had. His family and friends had been very helpful *after* the event—after they'd broken up.

His barns were heated for the worst of the weather, but today the space was warmed by the residual heat that had collected earlier in the day. JD dropped his arm, and immediately missed her closeness and wished he hadn't, which of course was another reason it had been a good move.

Obviously realizing they were somewhere different, Mia's head swiveled from side to side. Turning to Evie to share that, pulled him up short. She, too, was twisting from side to side, her face shrouded in wonder.

"This... this is *amazing*. I've always wanted to see inside a real barn, pet the horses. Can we? Can we pet them? I read once that a horse's coat is like satin. Is that right?"

At first, he didn't respond. Misinterpreting his surprise, she rushed on. "Oh, sorry. These are working horses, right? You don't want them touched? I know horses are really valuable. I had to research that for a takeover case."

He blinked, stalling for time so his head could catch up. "You want to pet them? You've never been up close to a horse?"

Wonder still shone from those eyes as she shook her head. Though it was hard to tell because she was still turning from side to side, appearing to want to take it all in at once. "Not many horses in the part of 'Frisco I grew up. The only ones I ever heard about were race horses, and then never in glowing terms. Possibly because it meant someone had lost money. Again."

JD tried to analyze what she'd just said. The picture she'd painted didn't gel with the one he'd had in his head, and he was reminded again how little he knew about this woman. That feeling grew as he continued to watch her, noting she'd suddenly looked awkward, almost embarrassed. Why? Was she sorry she'd spoken up? The need to know more about her instantly blew up inside him like a big old balloon, filling him, threatening him with its urgency. However, something warned him to go slow. Keeping it light had worked before.

"Darlin', if I brought a pretty woman—two in fact—into this barn and didn't allow them to slather love all over these animals, they'd make me pay for it, and it'd be painful. Come on over here. This one here is Sugar, and as you probably guessed she's just as sweet. She's Mom's horse, and I'm pretty sure she's sick and tired of having to deal with men all the time—missing having someone gentler around. Someone who smells a whole lot better than the rest of us."

Something odd flickered in her eyes when he said that; they darkened, softened… But then she turned back to Sugar, and it was gone. Though not without him suddenly yearning to see that look again.

Masochist. Yup. He was a masochist.

She was looking up at Sugar, who, while not one of the bigger horses in their stable, still towered over her. Awe still shone from Evie's eyes, but her hand he noticed, had stopped on its journey to touch the horse; fallen back to her side. Reaching over, he clasped it, shepherded it back, guided her. "Here, move to her from the side so she can see you. That way she won't take fright," he said softly. "There… See?

Stroke down her nose. She'll love that."

His hand covered hers, still guiding her smaller one, noting the slight quiver receding as Evie gained confidence. Noting that he liked holding her hand like this, liked helping her, teaching her. Not liking that he liked it.

And yes, it was becoming awkward, like a handshake held for that fraction too long. The fraction that turned something acceptable into something creepy. Would creepy feel this good though? Or maybe *she* was finding it creepy. The thought was enough to make him whip his hand away and merely watch.

And yes, watching could be creepy, too, but he couldn't exactly close his eyes. That would be even creepier and surely he had enough control not to cross that line.

"Oh…" It was more of an intake of air than an opinion or pronouncement. That pulled him up, worried for a moment that she'd read his thoughts, or that he'd actually been, you know, creepy. It was her expression that calmed him.

No, not about him, but about this experience, and JD couldn't stop the smile that unfurled, nor those nice feelings that stirred as he watched her face. He didn't think he'd ever witnessed raw emotion radiated so profoundly.

"What do you think? Feel like satin?"

"Yes," she whispered. "And power and might, and loyalty and pride and…" Her words trailed but the delight didn't diminish.

"Here," he said, scrambling in the pocket of his jacket. "Hold your hand out flat, and offer them to her. You'll be a friend for life."

Evie took the sugar cubes and yes, he saw wariness there as she did as instructed, laughing softly when her new friend nuzzled the treat right off her palm. Eyes alight she turned to Mia. "Look, beautiful girl. See this lovely horsie?"

JD released Mia from the pouch and turned her so she, too, could properly see the animal. Unlike Evie, the baby had no wariness to overcome, instead reaching her hand out to grab at Sugar, who instinctively turned her head, to rub gently against the baby's hand. Mia's exuberant little shrieks of joy didn't faze Sugar one bit, even when, obviously anxious for more contact, Mia reached out both hands, cupping Sugar now on each side of her long face. In turn, the horse stilled; didn't move a muscle until Mia pulled her hands away.

"Oh…" This time it was a definite pronouncement, and when JD turned to Evie, tears had filled her eyes. "That's so beautiful. It was like Sugar knew that she was dealing with a baby." Swiping at an escaping tear, Evie added, "Oh JD, Mia's going to love it here."

JD's mouth pulled in at the edges as those words washed over him. Did Evie even know how much she'd given away when she'd spoken those last words? This whole thing may have begun as a good deed for a needy friend, but it had been becoming more and more evident to him exactly what a wrench it would be when Evie had to finally say good-bye to Mia. His chest tightened and he pushed away the other thought that was trying so hard to forge forward and taunt him—that maybe *she* wouldn't be the only one to feel a wrench.

Time to derail that thought train.

"Animals have amazing instincts when it comes to most things," he began, politely ignoring her scrabble for a tissue and subsequent cleanup. "But especially with kids. Mom had four kids under six and she swears that the old collie dog we had, when we were kids, half raised us. Mom'd let Jack and me out into the yard while she had her hands full with Leo and Joey, knowing Winnie, the dog, would keep us out of trouble, or alert her if we didn't heed Winnie's warnings." He paused, caught still, by the light shining from her eyes. "How about you? Favorite pet?"

The smile disappeared so quickly it made him wonder if the sudden need to bury her face in the tissue she'd previously been scrunching had been deliberate. Her voice was muffled. "No, no pets." The chuckle she added was about as unconvincing as the current political candidate's promises. "No time. So, where's your horse? I figure you'd have a favorite?"

One quirked eyebrow was the only indication he offered that maybe he saw through the quick subject change, but if she'd noticed, she wasn't letting on. On a quick inhale, he nodded to the big doors at the other end of the space.

"Thataway."

Outside again, she leaned her arms along a corral rail that almost came up to her nose. Having only one hand free, JD reached it around her and hefted her up, holding tight until her feet found purchase on a lower rail, allowing her to see more easily. "There he is," he said, pointing to the furthest side of the corral. "His name's Raider, but trust me it should have been Casanova or Lothario."

Evie leaned slightly over the rail and he had to look away. That pert little behind was very distracting at the best of times, but almost impossibly so when it was protruding out right in front of him.

Still perched in his arms, Mia frowned and growled at him. The kid was way too intuitive.

"He's beautiful!" Evie stretched out her arm, calling softly to the animal who was studiously ignoring them.

"Don't get fooled into thinking he's as hospitable as Sugar. He's ornery, stubborn, and has a completely warped sense of humor. Right now, we're getting payback—being ignored—because I didn't take him out for a ride today. Thinks he's pretty clever too, as well as being God's gift to every filly or mare within whinnying distance. Shameless. Thinks he's just got to call and they'll come trotting over."

She flicked a cheeky grin across in his direction. "He'd fit right in then. Sounds maybe like some of the other Halligan men on this ranch?"

Stifling a grin, he said, "Considering I've been on my

best behavior, I'm left to assume you mean Jack? And you wouldn't be wrong. Leo, too—as you'll see when you meet him."

She rolled her eyes. "Only Jack and Leo? Come on now, JD. This isn't the time to be coy." The laughter in her tone called to him, but he played it cool. "Most people," she continued, "resemble their siblings way more than they realize. Behavior as well as appearance."

"Really? Been my experience that *most people* don't know what they're talking about."

"Ha! Or maybe they do. Psych 101," she tossed back over her shoulder. "One of my undergrad subjects. Apropos to that, it's been my experience that most people have no idea about how they project themselves either."

"Ha!" he echoed. "*Most people* who worry about what other people are thinking, are hiding something."

Surprise tinged her reply. "Psychology?"

"*Ask Agatha*, twelve midnight to one A.M., Monday to Thursday, Countrywide Radio."

Evie twisted fully to face him, looping her arms around the rail behind to steady herself. His groan was partially swallowed, hidden behind fussing with Mia. *Most people didn't realize when they were going to pop a strategically placed button, either.* Was this some kind of test of his self-control?

"*Ask Agatha?* Psychologically speaking you do know that that response said more about you than you maybe wanted to reveal, right?"

She was still laughing as she shot that comment across the bow, and that helped. Helped him a lot. Today had been the first time he'd really heard her laugh out loud. Heard her simply let loose, and it surely was a captivating sight and sound; made him want to laugh right along with her, releasing some of the tension she'd inadvertently provoked in him. Relief washing through him when she, thankfully, jumped down off the fence.

Now he just had to contend with the memory. And the ensuing fantasy that would follow.

Maybe that tension hadn't shut down at all.

Of mutual accord they began wandering back toward the house, "Yup, it says that I'm a poor overworked rancher in need of rescuing."

Her eyes fairly sparkled. "Awww… Agatha's not helping?"

Side-eying her, he chuckled. "Nah… She just left me hangin' in the wind."

"Cruel."

Laughter had carried her response, and his own grin was fast and sure. "That's it? No sympathy? No advice?"

"Okay…" She appeared to think about it for a moment. "Psych 101 would tell you that you need a diversion. A hobby. Maybe a girlfriend. Or wife."

His roaring snort made Mia jump and he quickly soothed her before continuing, but even then, there was no way he could keep the disbelief out of his voice. "You think having a partner is akin to having a hobby? Like woodturning? Stamp collecting? Sweetheart, that says a whole lot more about you than anything I've admitted today. What kind of warped relationships have you had?"

Evie was now laughing so hard she had to lean against him for support. "No," she finally managed, "I didn't mean that. It kind of came out wrong."

And he had to admit, he didn't mind that leaning one little bit, either. Just like he didn't at all mind being in this moment with her—her face all flushed, hair somewhat askew, eyes sparkling through tears of laughter. Didn't mind the warmth that spread through him, all sweet and syrupy, as he took it all in.

Didn't mind at all.

But it did scare him. All the way to hell and back.

Or should that have been *heaven*?

IT MUST HAVE been the fresh air. That was the only reason Evie would accept that could explain her sudden lighter mood when she'd awakened the next morning. Even the thought of the dozens of messages and emails that would await her didn't dim her mood—right up until the realization that they weren't there, and wouldn't be there. The shock that memory bought rattled her, scrubbed away some of the shine this new day had arrived with, and a sense of loss, of being cast adrift threatened to obliterate the rest.

Then Mia stirred; rubbed her tiny fists across her eyes, blinked then turned her head to find her. Evie stilled. Waiting for the moment the baby's eyes found her, and then the sun once more bloomed, even if only in Evie's heart, pushing away those other scary feelings, at least for the moment. All because this precious child had smiled at her—a smile filled with joy, love, and excitement.

Evie hadn't been the only one to sleep well. Mia had slept a little later and had hardly stirred through the night. In the baby's case, it could have been that she'd simply worn herself out.

After they'd returned to the house yesterday, she'd bathed Mia, and then given JD some tips on diaper changing—both she and JD deftly ignoring the irony of that situation—and it had all been a hoot until it wasn't. Just as she was learning the vagaries of Montana weather, so Evie was learning that babies' moods could also flip with little warning. Especially teething babies. Apparently.

Mia's irritated squalls had hit the rafters and bounced around the room, terrifying both the adults caring for her, until JD phoned Nan who advised some of the baby acetaminophen she'd packed in the infamous carton of goodies she'd supplied. The same carton Evie hadn't been able to bring herself to glance into.

Once more though, JD proved what a great uncle—and father—he'd be by helping out every step of the way. He'd held and jiggled and walked the floor with that baby for hours, taking turns with Evie. The difference was that while he'd remained calm, she'd fallen apart, assuming it was somehow her fault. That she'd failed Hope. Thankfully Nan had talked her off the ledge, warning that this wasn't unusual behavior, and this probably wouldn't be the only time.

Relief finally came for them all when the baby had eventually calmed, even managing a couple of heart-melting smiles before she'd fallen asleep.

And that's when things could have become awkward. *Should* have become awkward. She and JD had been deftly side-stepping the huge elephant in the room. She knew he was experiencing some kind of physical reaction to her, just as she knew of her own reaction to him. So then, finding themselves alone, the comforting aroma of pine filling the air as the open fire crackled and popped beside them, warming the room and warming their bodies—that elephant should have been charging at them, leaving them nowhere to sidestep.

Curiously, somehow it hadn't, and yet there was something... She'd put it down to them both being emotionally drained after their worrying episode with Mia, but it was more. There was not only relief when Mia finally settled, but a strange sense of accomplishment, not of being victorious exactly, but of a wholeness that filled her and warmed her from the inside. Sure, they'd high-fived when, soundly asleep, Mia had been placed into the crib, but she saw something else in his eyes as well. Something deeper, something she recognized as exactly what she, too, was feeling.

And in that instant, she'd known. It was the wholeness of working together alongside him. Of being part of something special and meaningful. Of caring for a little human who was helpless and vulnerable and fully reliant on them.

Of doing it all with *him*.

The arm he'd tossed over her shoulder as they'd wandered back downstairs to attack the mayhem they'd left there had felt warm and inclusive. Felt strangely right. The wine he'd poured had been welcome and soothing. And the stories he'd shared of growing up in this place, in this family were at times poignant and, at times, hilarious. They painted a picture of JD Halligan that she knew she would take home, held close to her heart.

And maybe for the first time, she truly began to question the life she had so carefully, so deliberately, chosen.

That wasn't helped when he walked her to her bedroom door later that night. Wasn't helped when he'd held her close. Wasn't helped when he pressed his lips, warm and soft, chaste—against her forehead.

Wasn't helped when she knew deep in her heart how much she'd wanted more in that moment. Wanted so badly to lift her face to his and read what was going on in his eyes; to show him what was in hers. To invite all that *more* that she'd craved.

In retrospect she shouldn't have slept at all. And yet she had, and felt all the better for it. Not fighting, no, *definitely not fighting*, the warm fizz of anticipation firing through her as she'd dressed Mia. The kind of anticipation that has your heart pumping just that bit faster, and causes your lips to continue to curve into a smile you seem unable to curb. The kind that makes you think you can scale mountains; take on the world.

The kind of anticipation that Evie had never before experienced. And it all revolved around JD Halligan. Because, she finally admitted on a gush of honesty, that's what she was excited about. Seeing *him* again this morning.

Her heart should have sunk at the admission. *Would* have a couple of days ago. But now? Now she'd just embrace the moment and build the memories that would hopefully help keep her warm in the months to come.

He was coming in through the back when she arrived at the base of the stairs, Mia in her arms. The baby squealed and held her arms out to him, and Evie experienced a teeny touch of envy when in turn, JD's whole face lit up. This whole journey had been about ensuring Mia would be safe and loved. And she would, Evie had no doubt. Though as they were the two things that almost every human being craved, was it so bad to wish for that for herself a teeny bit?

The devil on her shoulder wasn't letting her off that lightly; posing the question she had been astutely ignoring: was it only a general craving to be safe and loved? Or to be safe and loved by one specific man? A specific man who was at that moment playing airplanes with his tiny niece, rocketing her through the air, encouraged by her shrieks of laughter.

Skating in for a smooth landing, he pulled up facing Evie. "Morning." He indicated the bundle he was holding with a grin. "Seems we're seeing the return of Miss Congeniality?"

"She slept well, so I guess we just have to see how today pans out."

JD nodded. "And speaking of today, I have a plan." His gaze zoomed in, capturing hers—and holding—before breaking the hold with a cheeky eyebrow jiggle. Breaking the hold made no difference, and it took a herculean effort not to visibly shudder as smoldering heat coursed through her—and of course he had to go and wink, making her wonder why she even bothered. The man saw and knew way too much.

What's more, he'd continued talking without missing a beat. "We didn't take those photos you need yesterday, so after breakfast I propose we check on the horses again and then see more of the property. And I figure we might be able to fit in a picnic lunch down by the river too. What do you think?"

What did she think? *What did she think?* A picnic? By a river? *With JD*, an inner rebel voice added. It was the way her heart sped up at that thought that sobered her, and instead of her initial cartwheel response, she offered a smile and a quiet thank you. "That would be lovely. Can I do anything to help?"

The minute the words had left her mouth Evie regretted them. Had she really just offered to prepare food? To his credit JD let it go, however she didn't miss the way his mouth pulled in at the sides, as though stifling a grin.

"Got it all under control."

And he was true to his word. After breakfast and with advice for both she and Mia to wear layers that could be peeled off when it became warmer, he led them out to the truck, which he explained was already packed with all they'd need. He'd even secured a baby carrier into the back seat of the truck—probably the carrier from her rental car which she'd have to do something about—but this moment wasn't for worrying about mundane things like rental cars. That was tomorrow's problem. Or maybe even the next day's…

The shift she'd felt yesterday, this new easiness between them, carried over into the new day, and there was nowhere to hide from the fact that she liked JD Halligan. *Really* liked him. Liked being in his company. Liked being the subject of one of those sexy smiles. Liked when his eyes sought hers—and held—and her stomach twisted in the most excruciatingly wonderful way. Yes, she definitely liked that.

Mia reacted with the same joyous excitement as before when they reached the barn. Okay, so logically speaking, her little kicking legs, squeals, and reaching hands could simply speak to her sweet naiveté, but it seemed deeper somehow. Could a love of nature be inherited?

"Maybe she'll be a rancher when she grows up."

JD side-eyed her. "Nah. She's smarter than that—she'll be a vet, keeping all these critters safe and well."

Close enough to reach him, she shoulder-nudged him. "You saying ranchers aren't smart, cowboy?"

His chuckle warmed her, thrilled her. Again. His returning shoulder nudge though, that was the big one. It was like opening a door and freeing thousands of butterflies that fluttered and jiggled and teased as they caroused right throughout her body.

It should have sobered her, worried her, but she side-stepped all that and simply gave herself up to the sensations, lived in the moment. However, for her own sanity she moved subtly away, only a step or two; just out of reach.

Not that it helped much. It took no time to accept that even if she was on the moon, and he on earth that her body would somehow still feel his pull. Right then though, her real life in San Francisco felt so removed, it could well be the moon.

He didn't immediately answer, and she turned back to him, guessing instantly that her subtle shift away from him hadn't been subtle enough. He'd noticed. It was there in the slightly wistful lift of one corner of his mouth, of the sardonic lift of one eyebrow. It was there in his eyes. Clouded now with something she didn't quite understand, still they snagged hers, and held—an invisible gossamer net that held her captive—unable to pull away.

"Just the opposite." And yes, it was there in the way his voice had dropped to a soft growly rumble that again tiptoed down her spine, tightening his hold, teasing those raw nerve ends that she'd tried unsuccessfully to tame.

She shivered, and his head tipped back, those eyes now hooded as he continued, his voice still low, seductive... "Being a rancher hones certain skills. Like being intuitive to the needs of others; good with our hands." Whispering now... "We're known for our intense dedication to a task; knowing when enough is enough, and when to forge forward, push harder, for that little bit more. Not leaving a job half done." He paused. "Some might say that's damned smart."

Oh... Yes...

Had time stood still? Her eyes burned. How long since she'd blinked? An eon? And breathe. Surely she hadn't forgotten how? Maybe she had. Just like her mouth had forgotten to form words, or maybe it was that her head had forgotten how to formulate the words. But even if either of those was working, there was no way she could have forced anything past the dryness threatening to choke her. Her pulse hammered so hard she wondered if he could hear it as clearly as she could, but there was no way he'd miss the surge of color that suffused her. All of her. Not only color but heat; raging, fiery heat.

Belatedly she remembered to close her sagging mouth. Scrambling for those elusive words still posed a challenge she couldn't meet. "Th-that's… um, it it's um…good."

As their gazes held, his gradually softened. Amusement grew, accompanied by another quick eyebrow jag that could have held wry humility. Or not. "Good?" His head tipped back, his laughter filling the space. She watched that strong brown column; itched to reach out and—oh, not that. Or maybe…

It was Mia who'd again pulled her back to sanity, or some semblance of it. The baby, intrigued by her uncle's laughter as he held her in his arms, reached out to slap a soft chubby hand against that exposed throat, bringing his face back to her, which she rewarded with a gummy smile.

Despite envying the baby's freedom to touch at will, relief that the moment was broken flooded through Evie, and maybe through JD as well. Although when he casually tossed his arm over her shoulder to guide her to the next stall, she did wonder if he had any idea what he was doing to her.

Not that she could see.

He calmly continued as before, clicking away with his phone, taking yet more photos, insisting she be part of them, proffering that it would offer solace to Hope as she lay in her hospital bed. Would *he* ever look at them? Later? After she'd gone back to her own life?

The initial question came from nowhere, yet it was the extension of that question that sucker-punched her. Or maybe, more correctly, her reaction to it. Surely her own life was where she wanted it to be? What she'd worked so hard to achieve. So why had her heart sunk at the thought of returning to it? The question was redundant—much as she wanted to convince herself otherwise, her heart knew the answer. That her unsettled reaction to returning home was really about leaving here; this place. And even more precisely, leaving this man.

Chapter Nine

JD NOTED THE exact moment her mood changed. What he didn't know was why. Mia? Work? *Him?* Unexpected hope flared at that last thought and he brushed it away as an unlikely reason, although instinct warned him to let her be as he steered the truck down closer to the river and parked on a flat piece of land his family had been using for picnics for as long as he could remember.

He'd be a fool if he didn't feel the awareness pulsating between them; didn't see it in her eyes. But also, confusion, reticence. Shyness even? It made him wonder if she'd be a shy lover, whether she needed someone to free the passion he saw in her, someone to build her confidence, and—*hells bells!* He had to fight hard against the instant rush of fiery desire to be that someone, desire that tightened his jeans and had his heart thundering. Desire to stroke that satin soft skin, to bring her alive under his touch, to press his lips against every inch of her.

Pulling to a stop, he squeezed his eyes shut. Not daring a single glance her way as he fought for control. Forced his mind to other things—like taxes and mucking out stables and concerns about getting the herd down. Anything but her.

It almost worked. Deliberately losing himself in mundane thoughts he hoped would restore some kind of respectability, he stepped out of the truck only to have the gasp, loud and heartfelt that had reached across to him, take him straight back to her. This time, with both surprise and concern. One look, however, assured him that all was well.

Kind of.

One look that dredged up every fantasy he'd had about her; one moment that he would have happily frozen in time—and his own breath held.

Evie was a beautiful woman, he didn't need reminding of that—her golden beauty was like a beacon that drew him, had drawn him, intrigued him from the first moment he'd laid eyes on her. However, the expression on her face right then took his breath away. It elevated that beauty to something almost spiritual. Her eyes, wide and blue, shimmered with unshed tears impelled by the glow of sheer wonder that seemed to shroud her as she stood beside the vehicle, captivated by the view before her. Her lips, so soft and full, trembled and it took every ounce of self-control he possessed not to leap over the truck and gather her close, to still those lips with his own, to harness all that raw emotion and mesh it with his own.

He closed his eyes; forced himself to breathe. Fought for calm. Dared to move closer to her. Cleared his throat to steady his voice as he spoke, "Yup, it's pretty awesome. A view I never tire of." And, conceding even as he did so that they were definitely focusing on two very different vistas.

That observation had come straight from his heart. He would never tire of looking at this woman. Problem was, she wouldn't be here for him to gaze upon. So where did that leave him?

It took her a moment to turn to face him, surprise clouding her eyes momentarily, probably at finding him now so close. "It's magnificent." Her voice was soft, breathy. "You're so lucky to have this—" She spread her arms wide. "All *this*, on your doorstep."

He knew it, but as he faced the panorama, to view it again through her eyes, he knew that, for him, something had finally surpassed it.

He focused on the other one. Those majestic mountains, smoky, gray with shades of purple in the far distance. The brilliant white of their snow-capped peaks made even more startling by the clear blue backdrop of sky that went on forever. The breathtaking contrast of the golden aspens set against tracks of green pines, so stately, so serene. And then before them the river. A deeper blue than the sky, burbling along, the white caps that peaked and ebbed. "Like joyous, overly enthusiastic water nymphs who have trouble staying in line."

She tilted her head toward him. "Pardon?"

"The whitecaps. That's how my grandmother used to

describe them. Always. According to her, the bubbling sound is their chatter. I'd forgotten that until now."

Her responding smile made him forget a whole lot of other things as well. First and foremost, his own name…

"That's so sweet!" Her smile deepened. "I'll never look at whitecaps again without seeing mischievous water babies bobbing up and down, or hearing them happily call to each other."

It was only when her head tilted once more, and her smile began giving way to a frown, that he realized he was still staring at her. Captivated by her just as she was captivated by the natural beauty around them.

Turning quickly, he shook himself; attempted a reset. "So, we'd better get this little madam out before she begins complaining. We've got a picnic waiting for us."

They worked together to lay a blanket, set up cushions to support Mia, unpack the basket he'd provided and set up a small camp stove. "To heat Mia's bottle," he explained, catching Evie's curious glance.

"Definitely *uncle-of-the-year* material. You thought of everything." Eyeing the spread before them, she added, "Actually, you really have. How did you do all this? Not all by yourself?" *Maybe he had.* "Did you?"

He shrugged. "Kind of. I knew we had the fried chicken pieces in the freezer. Nan called late last night—to check on Mia—and we got talking. She met me halfway early this morning with fresh baked bread and some salad and fruit—

and ta-da! Wait for it..." He reached into a second basket she hadn't noticed. "This amazing apple pie! And she said Mia can have some of the apple filling—so we're set. All of us!"

Evie went to speak, but for some reason she seemed to be choked up and he forced a grin. "Apple pie. Gets us every time, right?"

"Every time..." The relief in her eyes at being given an out was brief, but not so brief that he missed it. What was it that had triggered such an emotional response? He was pretty sure it wasn't apple pie. Well, actually, maybe it was, but somehow, he didn't think so. What had she been thinking right then? Had the picnic stirred bad memories? Sad memories? Of happier times? She'd intrigued him from the get-go, but with each passing minute the desire to know more about her burned hotter.

Stretching out on his stomach, he leaned in close to Mia, entertaining her by wriggling her bunny toy, tickling her toes, while covertly shooting glances across at the woman sitting beside them. Mia responded to the game in the way he'd come to love and expect, and he chuckled along with her. He loved the sound of the baby's laughter almost as much as he loved—*Whoah*. Mentally, he pulled himself up. That was a big word to throw around, even if he really was only thinking about the woman's laughter.

"You're so good with her."

Blinking back those worrying thoughts, he cocked an

eyebrow. "High praise indeed from a thirteen-and-a-half-hour YouTube veteran. I thank you. I'd even humbly bow if I wasn't…" He indicated his prone position.

She rolled her eyes. "*Ask Agatha* would be so proud. Hey! Do listeners ever chime in on the problems? Offer their own advice? You could do that! Help someone having a problem with their six-month-old child; you could help Agatha!"

"A suggestion offered with such sincerity." Grinning, he pushed to a sitting position, warmed by her cheeky giggle, and handed over a plate.

They ate in silence for a few minutes but he could tell something was brewing. The darted looks he caught aimed across at him were speculative as she picked at a piece of chicken, and he braced himself.

"Could I ask a personal question?"

There it was. He nodded. "Everything's on the table."

"So," she began slowly. "Am I right in assuming you'd like children of your own one day?"

He quirked an eyebrow in response. "Sure. Of course I do. However, contrary to the behavior of my brother, I think it's prudent to choose the right woman first."

Her eyes flashed; he'd hit a nerve. "How do you know he didn't? How do you know Leo didn't choose Hope to be his forever girl?"

JD pulled his hat down lower to counter the angle of the sun. "Well, I guess he didn't take her with him." He shrugged. "That's a point right there."

She pursed those full soft lips and he had to forcefully drag his eyes away in an attempt to concentrate on her words. "Hope says he was coming back for her, and I believe her."

But he hadn't, had he? The words, unspoken as they were, still hung there between them. JD had always loved his baby brother; always stood up for him. Right then, though, in his mind Leo was an ass, and he'd better haul himself back home pretty fast. But then once Leo returned, that would mean Evie would also leave. He swallowed, so lost in the desolate feeling that had swamped him with that reminder, that he completely lost track of their conversation.

Evie hadn't. However, the next question didn't make him feel any happier. "So, this woman who'll have your children? Is there anyone in particular you're keen on?"

He didn't dare look across at her. Just in case… "Nah. No one." The lie fell from his lips so easily he almost believed it himself. Because the truth was too ludicrous to entertain.

"Really?" she began, "But if I'm correctly reading Nan's earlier comment, there seems to be a few contenders for that title right there in your hometown. So, what's stopping you?"

Good question. Another good question was why had his heart dipped as he'd listened to her response. Had he really expected her to put up her hand for the job? He shrugged off both her response and his own meanderings. "Just busy, I guess." It was easy to go with an obvious response; easier than admitting his vulnerability; his fear that he'd make the same mistake again.

Beside him, Evie didn't even try to hide her scoff, and he turned to her, one eyebrow raised. "What? And you're so different? Seems to me work has quite a hold over your life as well. Are you going to tell me there's a boyfriend or fiancé waiting for you back in San Francisco?"

Her face scrunched into the cutest pout. "No... But—"

"Thought so. And your excuse is?"

"Okay, same. But my situation is different from yours." *Different from most people.* "You have a whole town full of single women ready to break down your door."

He didn't hold back his own scoff. What was good for the goose his grandmother would have said. "You're saying that all the eligible men in San Francisco are blind as well as obtuse? Beauty, intelligence, smarts—successful. What else could they ask for?"

"Pedigree."

The word had been uttered so quietly JD almost missed it. Low and, what? *Bleak?* Curious, he turned to her, hoping for clarification, fascinated as a kind of sadness morphed quickly into horror but even as he wondered, her chin lifted and she shot his question straight back at him.

"And cowboys don't want those same things?"

The image of Samantha flashed, once more stirring memories he thought he'd buried, but grateful that those memories didn't precipitate the same feelings of betrayal and anger as they once had. "Cowboys? Ranchers? I guess we're looking for the same, but also maybe resilience and commitment."

Evie seemed to give timely consideration to his response. "Isn't that the description of every successful relationship, no matter who or where?"

JD nodded. "Sure. But maybe we cowboys need it in a slightly heavier dose." Mia, tired of the rusk, began to fuss, and while he scooped her up Evie reached to the camp stove to warm a bottle. "It can be tough out here on a ranch sometimes. More vulnerable to weather. Isolating. Long days." He quirked an eyebrow. "But it's also pretty damned fantastic most of the time and best place in the world to raise kids—it's a great life—but only if you really love it all."

JD handed Mia over and watched Evie's whole expression change as she looked down at the baby now in her arms. Gentle—like she glowed. Neither of them said much as Mia fed, her occasional leg pumps becoming lazier until her eyes closed and Evie removed the teat of the now empty bottle from that sweet little mouth.

Together they changed her diaper and made a little makeshift bed, a move that meant JD had to reposition himself closer to Evie.

His arm brushed hers as Evie shuffled to face him and it took him a minute to realize she was speaking again.

"Your mom loved it?" There was a wistfulness in her

tone as she'd asked the question, and his own heart, still excited by the contact, suddenly softened. He watched her trace patterns on the blanket with her finger, and the urge to slide that teeny bit closer and pull her to him became a fierce ache in his chest.

Swallowing it all back, he strove to appear casual. "Yup. She sure did. She was a city gal out here on vacation and the old man swept her off her feet—at least to hear him tell it, though she never denied it—and yeah, she fell in love with the Montana mountain life. Took to it like she'd been born here." The image of his parents, still so in love after almost forty years together, brought a wistful smile. "I think that's the secret. Sure, Mom loved it here, but more than that? She loved dad—and that's what makes it work; what makes the person stay and make it work. Commitment." He grinned. "How about you. Kids?"

Her eyes darted straight to Mia, softening as they roved over the sleeping baby. He watched, seeing her chest rise with the gulp of air she'd sucked in, the blink as though she flicked away a tear. And his own heart filled. "It's okay," he whispered. She was a natural nurturer.

Surprise stared back at him. Her eyes clouded, and a deep *V* formed between her neat brows. "I... I'm not—" Her words stalled; one hand flapped.

He gave her a moment, waited until she'd gathered herself, wondering whether it was wise to prod any further. "You okay?"

"Sure. Sorry, you caught me off guard for a moment." The smile she added brought the sun back into his heart, warmed him from the inside out, and without thinking he quickly captured it with his phone.

"Hey!" She lunged for the phone which, he, being faster, tucked behind his back. "We're supposed to be getting photos for Hope. She doesn't need another one of me," she finished on a laugh."

"It's for Mia." Even as the words hit the air he wondered if he should be worried about how easily untruths were slipping from his tongue. "So, she'll remember you." That thought caused his gut to twist, prompting his next thought; hoping he wasn't plunging her back into some unexpected emotional pit with his next question. "My turn."

Laughter fading, she paused and frowned. "Pardon?"

"To ask a personal question." He allowed a heartbeat before continuing, but it was long enough for shadows to cloud her eyes, for that sparkle of moments ago to diminish. Long enough for him to, again, wonder why. Long enough for something dark and primal to surge through him—an urge to protect her, to hunt down anybody who'd ever hurt her. Rocked by his own response, his voice was rough, broken—knowing even before he'd uttered the words that he was half dreading her answer. "After—After all this…will you stay in Mia's life? I mean, will you see her, or—?"

EVIE'S HEART SQUEEZED. It wasn't an easy one, but she'd been expecting something more painful. He'd misunderstood her response to the children question, and that wasn't sitting well with her. But, a little voice posed, did she still really feel the same? Had Mia changed her choices about motherhood? More to the point had JD changed them?

That thought was enough to make her head spin and the part of her that clamored for a definitive *no* was left wanting.

JD was still watching her, waiting, his eyes narrowed so it was difficult to pick up his thoughts. What answer did he hope to hear? With a shake of her head she applied herself to this latest question, her vacillation in accord with her previous thought. "I don't know... I mean, I'd like to, but I guess it depends on Leo. Maybe he won't want me around. Maybe he and Hope will want Mia to begin a new life with him and your family with no strings to the past."

Thoughts of Hope reminded her she hadn't yet had a reply to the photographs she sent off to her during the drive over, justifying that with the thought that her friend might have been resting—or having treatment. But fearing something way worse.

However, when she looked up his reaction to her answer was patently evident. Anger. Fast and hot. It was there in his eyes, in the tight pull of his mouth, the set of his shoulders, warming her. "Why would they want that?"

There were a lot of reasons. Shame topped the list. But, how could she explain that to someone who'd lived a perfect life?

He didn't wait for her answer. "What about your own family? Your parents, what would they say?"

He'd let the question hang and so many words rushed forward. However, as though caught in a traffic jam, they all stalled, none of them making it past her lips. It was a long-held habit, born out of disappointment, to keep her past private, and it had quickly become easier to be vague. She'd never sought sympathy, and would have settled for indifference, but the jokes had hurt. The dismissal. The judgment.

She pushed that aside. That was then. This was now, and this time, casual misdirection seemed wrong. Duplicitous. At first, she'd been happy enough for JD to have perceived her life to be very different to her reality. Perhaps, not *happy* but, in a weird way, *relieved*. She wasn't surprised by his appraisal—after all, didn't most people in her adult life assume something similar about her?

However, now, for the first time, it mattered that *this man* knew the real her. And if he laughed or scoffed? Well, it would hurt, but it would also help her to move on; to push JD Halligan out of her heart.

Easy to say…

"Evie?"

She lifted her eyes to meet his, and all she saw was concern. The lump that instantly formed in her throat wasn't going to help. "My family won't have an opinion at all, JD, because they don't exist."

His mouth opened but she held up a hand.

"This isn't easy, so let me say it. JD, I've let you believe I've had a life that couldn't be further from the truth. I could have—*should have* corrected you, but well, I guess I've spent my whole adult life trying to blot out my childhood—and if I can be really truthful, I kind of liked the life you'd assumed for me—liked it a lot, so I just let it ride."

She hauled in a deep breath, steadied herself. "My mother, when she was alive, couldn't remember who my father might have been. Her main focus in life was getting her next hit or trading food stamps for alcohol. I spent my childhood being shuffled from one foster home to another, so many I lost count. Hope was a girl I met when we were temporarily housed with the same foster family. We were ten and it was barely a year, but she became the only person I was brave enough to form a relationship with. Ironically, she was also the last…"

She heard him swear—it was hushed but that didn't make it any less fervent.

"People let you down… Didn't hang around…" The words were growled; not a question, just fact. One she couldn't refute and didn't bother trying. No relationship in her life had stuck—not even her own mother. It wasn't fun, but she'd always known it could have been way worse. She'd never questioned where her determination to have a better life had come from, she was only grateful it was there.

On a shrug, she continued. "We were children; we had

no control over our lives. Losing Hope hurt the most—she was different, the sister I'd longed for, and unlike so many others who even from childhood seemed destined to follow the pattern set by their parents. She didn't, *we* didn't want that—we wanted more and we were going to support each other. But then suddenly we were separated again. I hadn't heard from her in all those years—until I received that phone call a little over a week ago."

JD had gone very still. "And it took you back there? To that time?"

Evie rocked her head to the side. "It did, but not in a bad way. Memories with her were the happiest I'd had as a child. I was surprised, but excited as well. And then—"

"Evie, I—"

She held up one hand. "Stop. JD, if you're going to offer sympathy you can stop right now. I don't need your pity. I don't pity myself or feel sorry for myself. It's not ideal, and sure, there are times when I wished it was different, but it's just life. The hand you're dealt. It's what I do with my life as an adult that counts, and I'm doing okay."

Both his eyebrows rose at her clipped tone, his lips pursed. "I feel no pity for you." He shrugged, pulling his shirt tight across those powerful shoulders. "I'm in awe. You're a beautiful, strong, successful woman. What you've achieved… I can't even imagine how you accomplished what you have."

Memories of those times appeared unbidden and unwelcome, but blessedly diluted by his acceptance. *JD Halligan didn't care about her past?* That brought a lightness to her response; lifted her heart. "The usual. Three jobs, no sleep." She added a wry laugh, waved a hand, not bothering to mention her astute study of other successful women she'd admired—how they spoke, walked, held themselves, modeling herself after them so she, too, could take her place in their world. But not quite. Same but not the same. She'd learned the hard way there was a big difference between looking the part, even *being* the part—and being *accepted* as one of them. "Ancient history."

"But not so ancient that you'd ignore a plea from the past?"

An image of her friend's face, her terror, appeared unexpectedly; flipped her mood, tore at her heart. "Hope was special. *Is* special." Tears built, filled her eyes. *Tears for Hope.* She stiffened, determined to push them back but still one escaped, tracking a watery line down her cheek. She brushed it away, took refuge in the view. "And anyway, anyone would have done the same if they'd seen her eyes; her fear." Her words caught, tangled in her throat. "F-fear that her baby might suffer the same fate as we had; that history would repeat itself."

The sudden harsh intake of his breath camouflaged the sound of movement, but strangely she didn't flinch when she found herself suddenly in his embrace, and for once, she didn't let reason take over. She leaned into him, relishing the comfort, the touch, the comfort of connection with another human being.

But this wasn't any human being—this was JD Halligan—and no matter how distracted her head may be, her body remembered. And the body heat she'd found companionable comfort in began a subtle change, a slow smolder at first, picking up speed, building in intensity, burning through her, enveloping her, gaining intensity and momentum. A fire that spread, sparking whispers of awareness that broke through the dark mood of the moment, tiptoeing up her spine, igniting her need with each step, dragging her into the next vortex of sensation.

His hands moved, repositioned, stroked, robbing her of the ability to think of anything other than the need for those hands to be on her flesh. His arms tightened, crushed her against his hard chest, held firm. His scent filled her, his breath fluttered escaped strands of hair against her temple, sending her nerve ends into a frenzy. His lips gently pressed against her forehead, so soft, so… Oh Lord… One large hand cradled her jaw, turning her to him, his groan muffled against her hair.

Her heart picked up pace, the rapid tattoo keeping time with the throb of need that hammered through her entire body.

Logic struggled for a voice, struggled through the haze suddenly encasing her. She couldn't deny she wanted this, *craved this*, but did she want it *like* this? *Because he felt sorry for her?* She should pull away, stop… Her hands came up to press against his chest, but his own hand moved to gently cover one of hers.

His mouth moved to her ear, his voice raspy, his words shuddering through her, "Do you want me to stop?"

This was the moment. Did she? *Did she?*

Hell no…

Her hands moved to cup his face, pulling it closer, bringing his lips to her, boldly taking his mouth, driven by the sudden desire raging through her. That first touch was electrifying, so firm, so soft. So generous. That first taste so decadent, sweet and salty at the same time—like warm caramel, so tempting and oh so forbidden.

But?

She heard the quick intake of his breath, felt it through her, empowering, obliterating any negatives, deafening her to her own insecurities. Not today. Not now. Today, rich flowing caramel was her favorite.

The tip of her tongue boldly darted forward, outlining his mouth, rewarded when the touch sent a frisson through him that shuddered against her own body. His arms tightened around her, crushing him to her against the muscled length of him as he lay pressed against her, masterfully taking charge, deepening the kiss, demanding more and more, beyond what she thought herself capable of giving. And yet she found it; gave him more and demanded more in return.

Closer. The word whispered through her thoughts. The

need swelled inside her, inciting, insistent, and she obeyed, shuffled her body slightly, turned further into him. His hands gathered her in, roved—stroking her back, cupping her bottom, pulling her even tighter, allowing her to feel his throbbing response.

Emboldened, her hands followed suit, molding those magnificent shoulders, stroking his face, his chest—thrilled by the stampeding heartbeat that thundered in time with her own. They tangled in his hair, drawing him in, swallowing the groan that seemed to come from the deepest part of him.

Still his lips plundered. Her nipples hardened, called to him and as though replying, his hands instinctively found her breast, finding those buds even through her shirt, rolling them, teasing them until she thought she would scream if those hands didn't soon tear away the protective covering; if his wonderful mouth didn't soon lavish them with the attention they craved.

Her stomach twisted, the throbbing in her lower abdomen grew to a crescendo and she squirmed to rub herself against him. It was the kiss she'd fantasized about, dreamed about, ached for… The one she knew she should never seek, yet right then, she couldn't think of a single reason why this shouldn't continue. Not a single one.

Maybe because this wasn't merely a kiss. It was a meeting of bodies and souls; of hearts. It was deep and warm and passionate and spoke to her in a way that words would struggle to convey. More… It was an answer. An answer to a question asked, and a promise made the first time they'd laid eyes on each other. Or maybe when she'd first laid eyes on him.

Who cared who asked and who answered? She was floating, dazed. Even the air around them seemed to stand still. Or maybe she was so engrossed in the feel of him, in the feel of *them*, that nothing else penetrated. This kiss could go on forever. Clinging to him, she *wanted* it to go on forever. To never stop.

But then it did.

His mouth moved from hers, it grazed her temple, his groan raspy and untamed against her ear. His hand left her breast, and she moaned, whimpered, when he pulled slightly away. Her eyes opened as she slithered to close the gap to recapture that warmth, and there was his gorgeous face, right above her. So near…

"We shouldn't do this." The words were choked.

She understood. "I know…" And she did. So why was she again reaching for his face? Reaching to pull him back to her?

Breathing hard, he caught her hands with one of his larger ones, and stilled them, his gaze catching and holding hers with the same surety. Burnt-caramel eyes searched her face, her own struggle with desire and sense mirrored there. "Evie, I don't think I can do this. Not and then just let you walk out of here when Leo comes back."

"But I want—"

"I know. So do I, darlin'." Lifting her fingers first to his lips, he then placed them down gently, allowing him to shift, adjust himself. "And I think you felt how much. But we both have to be honest here. Not only do I not have protection right now, this can't lead anywhere. We both know that."

Do we? His surety stunned her. But surely he was right? In days, perhaps only hours, they would go their own ways, resume their own lives. Nothing could come of a union between them. *Except the most exquisite memories to hold; to keep curled in her heart...*

Pulling to a sitting position she wrapped her arms around herself, chilled now that his body was no longer pressed into hers; her mind furiously scrambling for logic.

Problem was, it wasn't only her body suddenly feeling so bereft. It was all of her. Her body, her head...her heart. One thought bravely waved from the sidelines, and though she valiantly tried to scoff it away, it persevered; taunted her—chilled her.

No... Surely not?

Had she really been fool enough to let this place, *this man* and his life seduce her into beginning to believe there could be a different life for her? That she could have what others took for granted? That she'd found someone she could trust; someone who would finally stay?

Why now? Why this man? Was this some kind of mountain madness? She didn't have to look across to see him. He was there in her head, soul deep, imprinted on her, *in her*.

They'd known each other for a mere moment. Yet she knew him better than anybody else in her entire life. Knew his smile, his laughter, his kindness, his values, his honesty—even if that honesty, like now, tore at her. *And I can never unknow him.*

She wanted to be mad; to rage about injustice at her own body's betrayal, but instead, where an icy chill had just dampened her ardor of moments before, now heat surged again. Not the passionate kind, the mortification kind. Mortification at what she'd almost done; at what she'd almost revealed to him.

Revealed what she had only just realized herself—that she was falling in love with JD Halligan.

Chapter Ten

THE AIR HAD cooled and they'd made the unanimous decision to head back to the house. But the drop in temperature had nothing to do with the chill deep inside him. He'd messed up. He wasn't sure how, just that she'd pulled away. Hadn't he simply been the voice of reason? Their lives were polar opposites. It would never work. *They* would never work.

After Samantha, he'd determined any future relationship would have full disclosure. No secrets. Of course, he ignored the fact that, strictly speaking, this—whatever was happening between him and Evie—was not, *technically*, a relationship. Well, it was, but not in the romantic sense. Though, how in hell was he to try to define it otherwise—or define it at all!

He hadn't needed the extra brain bruising and instead focused on trying to get her to talk. Surely, he'd only stated what they both knew? Maybe he'd judged her wrong, but she didn't seem like the *fling* type of woman and he thought he was saving her from regret.

God help him—there was no saving himself from the regret that they hadn't continued. He knew what he had done was right, but that didn't mean it was easy. The paradox there was that never had anything in his life ever felt as right as holding this woman and making love with her. He wasn't really poetic, but there was a sense of homecoming he would be hard put to explain. The way her body had responded to his, her unexpected boldness, her sweet surrender. Not only her, but them. *Them together.*

And dammit it had just been a kiss!

No, it wasn't, and never would be, *just a kiss.*

It had been something magical and he wasn't too proud to admit he'd never experienced anything close to that, never felt so at one with a partner, never felt so welcomed and so... There was that expression again: home. Like he'd come home.

The truck juddered, and her eyes flicked across at him, momentarily filled with alarm, before he righted it, apologized for scaring her. Truth was, it had happened because he'd scared himself.

Because in that moment before he missed steering around that deep depression in the road, he'd been temporarily blinded by one searing fact—they hadn't been on the brink of sex.

Sex was great. Fabulous. Awesome.

What they'd shared had promised to exceed that. Was this what the term *making love* really meant? Had they been about to embark upon—? And what in the hell did that even mean? He swallowed the curse that bubbled.

The thing was—whether he let her walk away, or begged her to stay, the outcome would be the same. Heartache.

And even if he begged, would it make a difference? She had a life in San Francisco, one she'd worked even harder for than he'd ever imagined. Not only would he be risking his heart, he'd be denying her of her dream.

No, the facts remained that soon she'd return to her life in San Francisco and he'd stay here—and what? His gut twisted. Stay here and pine for her? Not that there was much choice. Pining or heartbreak? At least pining left him with good memories—and he closed his eyes to block out the rest of that sentence—*good memories and a lifetime of sleepless nights.*

Heartbreak however, often came with resentment. His mind flashed to Samantha for backup. Yep, no good memories there.

He dared a glance across the truck's cab at Evie, still focused on her phone. She'd shut him out. Not in a schoolgirl, sulky way. No, Evie Davis had more class than that. She'd smiled sweetly and made polite, inane conversation, answered when he'd asked—as long as it was all mundane. Twice he'd tried to deepen the conversation; twice she'd frowned him off with a worry that she hadn't heard from Hope and turned to her phone. He wasn't discounting that worry, it prickled his concern, as well—but he recognized diversion when he saw it. Her point was clear—she wasn't going to be drawn into sharing what was really eating at her, and he had no choice but to go along. For now…

It was evident when he pulled into the yard that they weren't alone. Nan wasn't sitting in her car, and there was no surprise when they found her inside enjoying a coffee beside the fire she'd lit in preparation for a cool night. Eyes that had seen too much for all of his life flicked back and forth between him and Evie as they'd thanked her for the pie, each stumbling over words that should have been easy.

Taking the coward's way out, JD gallantly offered to see to Mia, and slipped upstairs. It wasn't an escape as much as a temporary reprieve, time for him to prepare himself. Because, no matter what was going on in Nan's head—and he could see there was plenty—she'd go easy on Evie, whereas *he* was sure to be the recipient of all of it as soon as she had him alone.

SILENTLY CURSING JD for being quicker off the mark to grab Mia as an excuse, Evie followed Nan's suggestion and made herself some coffee before settling on the sofa across from the older woman.

Nan nodded to Evie's clothes, to the skintight jeans, the soft flannel long-sleeved shirt with its stripes of baby pink and cream—something she'd never have chosen but somehow had fallen in love with. "Suits you. Those pretty colors sit well against your skin. Brings out a kind of glow. Of course, other things can bring about a glow, but that shirt doesn't hurt, it just helps."

Evie's mind immediately went back to earlier, to her and JD, so recently entwined in each other's arms. She closed her eyes, to try to block out the images, sure that now she'd opened that floodgate again, a rush of heat would follow, rosy pink heat. Opening her eyes, she was sure she detected a twinkle in the other woman's, but if so, it disappeared and Evie relaxed a teeny bit.

Nan reached down to pull wool and needles from a bag beside the sofa that Evie had only just noticed. Baby clothing? She watched as her companion expertly began clicking the needles with a melodic rhythm that Evie had long been fascinated with but had never mastered herself, perhaps partly because knitting, with no one but herself to receive the end product, hadn't lived up to the romantic image in her head.

"So, how's Mia? Okay today?" Nan continued. "I had to be out this way and thought I'd drop in and check on you all."

Reminders of the night before produced a heartfelt sigh. "We were so grateful for your help last night, Mrs. Turner."

"*Oh, tosh.*" Nan shrugged away Evie's gratitude. "And call me Nan." She barely paused before forging on. "Babies can be such a worry. But I've always found that the most important tool is simply caring. That's the main thing. The second is to seek help and advice if you're unsure. You pair did both, so you excelled. Top of the class!" She chuckled.

"Just think of it as great experience for when you and JD have your own babies."

Coffee literally sprayed through the air, and Evie had to move to ease the coughing as her ensuing gasp followed the spray. "W-what? JD—*and me*? No, no... I mean... It...it was just a kiss... No, I mean... Just no."

While Evie struggled for composure, Nan continued knitting, and even as she hated herself for making the comparison, the fictitious Madam Defarge of Dickens version of the French revolution came to Evie's mind—though she'd never think of Nan Turner as a hag. Cheeky and mischievous, though? Definitely.

"Oh darlin'—I didn't mean that! I just meant when you and or JD ever have children. Either one of you, independently. Heaven forbid that I would embarrass you like that."

There was absolutely nothing to refute or object to in those words, yet Evie was left with the distinct impression that Nan had meant exactly what she'd first implied. Especially when she detected that smug little smile very cutely defining the impish expression on the older woman's face.

It was the smile that brought Evie down off the ceiling beams, steadied her heartbeat. Nan was just a sweet older lady playing matchmaker for someone she loved. Though why she'd think Evie was a likely choice was a mystery. Still, it was hard to take offense.

Nan continued knitting as though completely unaware

of any turmoil Evie was experiencing. "Actually..." Evie frowned at the change in Nan's tone. "I'm glad to have you alone for a moment, Evie. You see, I think I owe you an apology."

Curiosity prompted Evie to study Nan's face closely but even as she watched, one thought, the only thing Evie could think of connecting Nan and herself, came to mind and once more brought yet more color to her own. Goodness me—at this rate she could hire herself out as a STOP sign! Waving away the promised apology was as much for herself as for Nan. Did the woman really expect her to discuss those *gifts*? "It's okay. Really."

Nan scuffed one boot against the other, her eyes downcast. "No, I was out of line. I love these Halligan kids as if they were my own, and we have a very liberal relationship. I put those things into the box more as a joke for JD than anything else, but after I saw the way he looked at you—and you at him—I decided to leave them in the carton."

Evie spluttered. "Pardon me? *The way we looked at each other?* I—"

The older woman smiled—that knowing smile Evie was becoming way too familiar with. A smile that brought more heat to Evie's face. Instinctively she brought her fingers to her lips, imagining she could still feel the pressure of JD's against her own. Pressure that made her lips tingle and set fire to every other part of her body, with even just the memory reigniting the pulsing throb down low and her tummy to curl and drop in the most delicious way; made her body soften, ready itself...

Before her, Nan shuffled, moved—did something—and whatever it was had the same effect as being doused with cold water. Eyes wide Evie snapped her attention back to the older woman whose smile was now, impossibly, even more knowing.

Mortified, Evie's face blazed, this new fire making a mockery of her earlier embarrassment. "I—er, I..."

Nan's chuckle brushed away the need for explanation but it didn't relieve Evie's discomfort. The woman's eyes, that chuckle...

"Darlin'," Nan began, "there's no need to feel awkward. It's life and it's what makes it keep spinning round. And I couldn't be happier for you both. Something tells me you haven't always had it easy, and JD? That boy's heart was near crushed when that woman hurt him so. His mama and I feared he'd close himself off, and for a while that's exactly what he did. Now, I've only seen him a couple of times since you arrived on the scene, but even so I'm seein' a different man. I'm seein' some of the old JD—the one who laughed and enjoyed life."

Evie couldn't drag her eyes from Nan's face. Her own awkwardness had melted away as Nan spoke, replaced by a mix of deep sadness and wild curiosity. "JD was hurt by someone? A woman?"

Nan nodded. "A woman who was his fiancée. They were

set to get married and then it all blew up. I'm not saying we weren't hurting for him. But there was relief there as well. Samantha wasn't right for JD—we all saw it. All but him. But thankfully he came to his senses. Problem was the cost..."

Samantha? "The cost?"

"Uh-huh. The cost to JD's soul. It's bound to happen when trust is broken, but JD seemed to take it harder than others might. But of course, that's because he's such an honorable man; a respectful man who speaks the truth and expects that others live by the same moral code."

Evie's head was spinning. "Can I ask—"

Nan's upraised hand brought Evie's question to a floundering halt. "Please don't ask me for specifics. I've already said too much. It's his story to tell—or not." The words were uttered quietly, her eyes now turned to the man in question as he wandered back into the room carrying a blinky-eyed, rosy-cheeked baby still half cocooned in the vestiges of sleep.

BACK IN HIS truck only a few minutes later, JD darted a look across at Evie, head back, staring out through the windscreen. He wasn't sure if she'd recovered from what had happened earlier, or whether it was merely temporarily replaced by a new worry, but he was grateful for the change he felt in her.

Her head lifted, frowning as she looked across at him.

"Are you sure that woman isn't a witch? How have we let this happen? One minute we're all sitting around playing nice and the next, you and I were being bundled off to enjoy *a little break from all the parenting*!" She shook her head. "Without Mia!"

"She's in good hands. Nan's a great mother—as well as a trained nurse. And she sorely misses her own grandbabies who live out in California. Other than my own mom or Doreen, there's none I'd trust more."

Her gaze darted across at him again, then scooted away, down to her hands that were twisting every which way. "Does it," she began softly, "does it show that much?"

"Yep." He deliberately kept his eyes on the road. "Evie—"

"I know, I know." Her hurried words cut him off. "I'm not stupid, I'm thinking the exact same thing I assume you're thinking. If I'm like this about leaving Mia for a couple of hours, how will I be—?"

Her breath hitched, pushing her into silence, and he slid a hand across the bench seat. He wasn't sure whether she'd meet him halfway, but she did, and the rush of emotion almost made him giddy. It was so much more than the touch of her satin soft skin against his, more than that his large hand dwarfed hers, more than that she brought out every protective instinct than he'd ever guessed possible—it was somehow symbolic. She'd met him halfway. He had no idea what deeper meaning he wanted that to symbolize, but it still made him want to beat his chest like some primitive caveman.

Made him want to pull over and drag her to him, beg for a replay of the kiss they'd shared that afternoon. A kiss that had stirred a depth of emotion so powerful it almost hurt. Had it been the same for her? He hadn't been able to get it out of his mind; hadn't been able to get *her* out of his mind. Nothing new there. Evie Davis had filled his every waking—and sleeping—moment since the minute he'd clapped eyes on her.

His mind jumped back to that day; he wanted to blame that damned sexy business suit, but it had been her eyes that had snagged him, and held him captive ever since. That woman, determined, aloof, professional—a woman wrong for him in every way imaginable.

Yet now he sat holding that woman's hand across a car seat, desperate to be holding all of her, arguing with himself that this had to be enough.

They were nearing the edge of town and though he hated severing that connection, he needed his other hand. She released it with the lightest squeeze, her smile shy.

"Pretty town. Pretty name—*Marietta*." Glad she had something to distract her, he focused on the cross street as she studied the homes they passed. It was more than idle interest, he could tell that by the way her head swiveled, but even he was surprised when she suddenly straightened, leaning forward. "That's her!"

"Who?"

"Her! A woman I saw when I was coming into town. Your cousin is with her."

Frowning, JD turned to follow her hand now pointed at a house a few doors along. A woman stood in the yard, a child clutched to her chest, and yes beside her, but not too close, stood his cousin Cody. "That lady? That's one of Cody's properties, so I'd say at a guess that's his new tenant." He turned his eyes back to the road. "He's guessing she's had some trouble. Seemed pretty anxious; needed someone to cut her a break, and Cody's stepped up." He glanced across. "You know her?"

"No. I only saw her once but there was something so desolate about her. She's kinda stuck with me—in my head. I'm glad Cody's helping her."

He nodded. "It's a sad fact that trouble is always saddling up a fresh horse somewhere, but Cody will see her right."

She fell silent after that, and he wondered what she was thinking. Had the plight of the woman stirred bad memories?

He'd parked and was out of the truck before he thought to ask what she felt like—and also late in figuring their attire hadn't given them a lot of options. For some reason that irritated him, quickly rationalizing by reminding himself this wasn't exactly a date. It was just a bit of time out; an opportunity for Evie to see some of the town before she moved on. Hitching his thumb back over his shoulder, he said, "Greys Saloon should be fairly quiet now. We'd beat the dinner crowd. It might not be what you're used to, but...?"

A frown fluttered across her eyes before she replied. "It looks great!"

Not a date, he reminded himself. So why was he suddenly feeling as awkward as a sixteen-year-old, seemingly too jittery to sit even after he'd secured them a table? "Ahh, I-I'll get the drinks. What would you prefer?" The words were no sooner out than he wished them back in, knowing his scowl wasn't helping to soften his next words. "Ahh hell... I should have thought this through... Look if you'd rather we go somewhere else?"

Clear blue eyes gazed up at him, her confusion evident. "Why?"

Hauling in air he pulled out his chair and sat, wondering how to delicately continue, especially when delicate wasn't his usual style. "Well, your mom...and her problems... I should have been more mindful. I—"

One soft hand reached across to him, found his own and pulled it closer to her, before covering it with her other hand. "It's okay." Eyes upon him, her voice was soft, low. He may not have mastered delicate, but she was all that. One thumb began stroking the side of his hand, a rhythmic caress, and he stilled. Such a simple connection and yet, nothing could have persuaded him to move a muscle. He felt her touch burning through him, like she'd ignited a fuse that sizzled, and buzzed through him from that spot, taking him back to earlier in the day, when she'd lain in his arms—

"Thank you." The words somehow penetrated the haze that had kept him captive. Not just any erotic haze, but one created by her and her alone. He blinked, tore his gaze from their clasped hands—only to drive it straight to hers.

Be captured by hers. Held to her gaze by invisible silken threads, mesmerizing him.

Breathe. Surely his body had forgotten how.

Her eyes shimmered with gratitude, brimming over, lighting her from within—for him? *Grateful to him?* Her beauty could never be questioned, but in that moment she was almost luminescent. Glowing. And if he ever remembered to breathe, he knew he would want to spend the rest of his life doing whatever it took, simply to have her gaze on him like that again.

He did breathe. But too hard and too fast. Clamping his jaw tight might have helped control it. Dragging his eyes away from her certainly hadn't. Her face was still there, front and center in his head, and now accompanied by a whole montage of images—all of her. Evie. *Gazing upon Mia with such love; determined, in wondrous awe, confused, pained, grieving, laughing, teasing, alight with passion...* His curse was silent and aimed at none but himself as the truth that he'd been so arduously refusing to see smacked him right between the eyes with an invisible fist driving it home. Hard.

Disbelief robbed him of all speech. Not disbelief that he'd fallen in love with her, *yes love*, but that he'd allowed it to happen.

And where in the hell did that leave him now?

❦

FOR SOME REASON, JD appeared to be discomfited by her gratitude, but she determinedly forged on. Her reaction to his question wasn't about drinks or alcohol, but about respect—consideration. "Alcohol was my mother's weakness, not mine, but again, thank you so much. I'll never be a big drinker, though. I've lived through too much of the other side for that. Even through work."

He took an age to respond, gather himself, and she wondered if she'd bored him, blinking when he seemed to shake himself back to the present. She watched as he cleared his throat, noting that the hand she'd clasped was now engulfing hers. "You—ah—don't like the social part of your job?"

Her eyebrows lifted. "Did I really reveal that much?" Her chuckle seemed to loosen something in him and he grinned back. "No, not my favorite part."

"What is your favorite part?"

Surprise robbed her of a direct answer. "I... er..."

He winked. "How about you think about it while I get those drinks. Coffee? Wine? Something else?"

Was it being here with him? Just him? Them together? Or was it perhaps the spurt of confidence his insightfulness had sparked? Whatever it was, she suddenly felt quite bold. Her gaze took in the typical wooden furniture, tables that could tell so many tales. The long bar, backed by dozens of sparkling bottles in an array of tempting colors, and serviced by patient bartenders who'd probably mopped a million tears. The retro jukebox—now providing a soundtrack of country crooners—and a floor that had seen more than its share of scootin' boots, and would no doubt stand up to all that again and more to come.

"You know, when in Rome so to speak…" She flashed him a smile. "I'm in a Montana bar with a hot Montana cowboy. I think I'll have a beer!"

"Hot, huh?" His amused surprise was right there in his husky laughter, in his one raised eyebrow. "I never argue with a smart lady—especially a lawyer. I'll be right back."

The pause, though brief, was welcome. Had she really choked at his question about her work? Why? She loved her work! *Didn't she?* She pressed Play on an internal video of her years with B,B&T, reliving the highlights. The suspense, successes, adulation—the long hours it took to realize those outcomes. Hours that she'd prioritized over any kind of personal life; choosing to do that to fulfill her goal.

By the time JD returned to their table, much of the bounce had gone out of her mood. As insightful as ever, he kept his eyes upon her as he placed the mug of froth-topped amber liquid in front of her, before resting his own identical glass on the other side of the table. "You okay?"

She nodded. Managed a half smile.

Narrowing his gaze he said, "I think we were talking about your work. Did you remember what you love about it?"

Yes, there was a touch of sarcasm in his tone, but she could hardly blame him. She'd been the one who'd stalled on the question. "Well, that's the thing," she began quietly, "I thought I loved everything."

"You sound like you're talking in past tense. What changed?"

He watched her closely and she bent her head to try to hide the sudden flush that was creeping up her neck and flowing over into her cheeks. The answers lined up in her head. *You! Mia! Nothing!* And everything... "I'm not sure." The fabrication came easily, cloaked in a veil of self-protection. "I became a lawyer to do right in the world—"

He lifted his glass, toasted her silently then took a sip. "Noble ideal. So, are you?"

"Making a difference? Doing right?" She frowned. "I guess I could try to sugarcoat it, justify it, but the raw truth is that I'm probably not doing what I intended to do with my life. It's mostly mergers and big-time takeovers. Mega money swallowing big money."

"And that's how you see your life continuing?"

"You know, this is starting to sound like a therapy session." She took a quick gulp, trying to stem the irritation that had begun to grate. She knew how her admissions were sounding, but he had no idea how hard she'd fought to have this life, and it wasn't his place to judge, closing her ears to the little voice whispering, *"Even if he might be right?"*

He lifted both hands in the traditional sign of surrender. "Sorry. I didn't mean to interrogate you. I just think it would be a crying shame if someone like you with so much to give sold herself short. I guess I wanted—" he paused, dropped his voice low, "I guess I just hope you have a happy life. You deserve it, Evie."

His admission caught her breath, smoothed out her irritation, warmed her—and that annoying burn at the back of her eyes warned she was about to show exactly how much. Swallowing past the accompanying tightness in her throat, she drew in calming air. There'd been few people in her life who'd cared enough to want anything for her, but that wasn't why it touched her so deeply. It was because it was coming from him. From JD Halligan. A man who made her yearn for things she'd long ago decided were not meant for her; who'd forged a crack in her armor and let her glimpse another life—one she would never have.

"I'm the one who's sorry. I—"

He winked across at her again, silencing her, and once more her insides began shimmying. How could one man, one mere human, have the power to do that? To flip her mood? To turn her to mush?

"Let's put that one away. And in the spirit of fair trade, I give you permission to put me on the spot. Ask me anything!"

His eyes sparkled, the innate cheekiness that so often drew her, was once more gleaming across at her. Daring her.

And a thought that had laid patiently waiting since her conversation with Nan raised its hand. He was daring her. But, *dare she*? Really? Running her tongue across her lips gave her a moment to reconsider, but crossing her fingers, she ignored it. "Have you ever been close to marrying? Engaged?"

Her heart dropped as that sparkle faded; his eyes narrowed, deliberately looking anywhere but at her as he took a long slow draught of his beer. A bowl of fresh nuts was delivered, and he thanked the server. Still, he avoided her. Would he answer? Would he deny it? Evie hadn't realized how tight she'd held herself until he began speaking.

"Once. Her name was Samantha. We were engaged, and then broke up. Lucky escape."

That was it? "That's it?" The words were slightly slower than her thoughts as she scrambled to identify how she felt. Disappointed? Worse—cheated?

He swallowed, shifted his glass, tracing circles in the moisture it left on the table. On a sigh that came from way down deep, he shook his head. Closed his eyes. "You're right. I'm not being fair. You shared your story and I owe you mine. I guess I've just never actually told a soul what really went down."

He took another gulp of the beer that was now almost all gone. "I'll try to keep it short. She was a city girl—beautiful—or so I thought. Funny how discovering the truth about a person alters how you see them." His delivery held no emotion, his tone pragmatic. His pause was filled with the sound of his hand being rasped across the golden whiskers that shimmered under the lamplight, and perhaps the only hint that maybe this was difficult. "We met over a property deal. Her company had their eye on some mountain land I own that they wanted for a resort, and she was sent to make the deal. The deal wasn't of my making and it failed, but she stuck. Claimed to love me and want a family to raise right here, and I thought I was one lucky man. Of course, I overlooked a lot that others didn't."

"Such as?" The prompt was gentle and she hoped would keep him on facts and away from the emotion that she suspected lurked under his stoicism.

"Oh, that for someone who loved this place as much as I did, she never wanted to be here. And when she was, she complained about everything. Wanted changes. Basically, what she wanted was for me to sell up and live with her in Chicago. She'd apparently get me, my money—and partnership in an eventual resort which would keep her in luxury for the rest of her life." He blew out a breath and shrugged. "To be honest I'm not even sure how long she intended to keep me as part of the deal. She assured me after everything came out that she really had feelings for me, just not my life or any part of my dream."

"I'm so sorry. That must have hurt…"

He shook his head. "I could have probably dealt with that, walked away. It was the other lie she told that crushed me." He looked up at Evie, and she read the betrayal so clearly, it literally took her breath. "I'd made it clear that I wanted a family, and she was on board, or so I thought. I believed her. Right up until I learned she'd been pregnant with my child."

"Oh no…" Images of him with Mia sprang to mind, of the love for a baby niece he hadn't known existed a week ago, and how he'd given her his heart, his protection, and her own heart twisted for him, dreading what was coming.

"She claimed she'd lost the baby naturally, and maybe she had, but that didn't explain why she'd chosen not to share the news with me, and wouldn't have if I hadn't found out—or why she'd scheduled a sterilization operation following the supposed miscarriage."

The room seemed to stand still, which was ridiculous. They were in a public bar, yet Evie's gasp echoed around them. "How—"

"Fate, I guess." He shrugged. "A text wrongly sent to me instead of a girlfriend." Evie watched as he relived that moment. Jaw clenched, fists tightened on the table. "She was making jokes about it." Suddenly, as though he was closing a door on it all, he leaned back into the chair, his expression again matter-of-fact. "She'd never wanted kids; had no intention, and presumably was going to spin some yarn about being infertile after we'd married. You know," he looked up, "I'm not saying not wanting kids is wrong, but it was the duplicity, the blatant lies."

"Oh, my Lord." Her head was buzzing, absorbing his story; her body hurting for him. "I'm so sorry. That must have dug really deep." The words were whispered, and she prayed they conveyed her true sincerity. She really was sorry he'd had to experience that, and for so many reasons; some of which were too personal. "And since? You've never?"

She let the question hang, realizing as she did that this was as much torture for her as for him reliving it all. She'd wanted to know what had hurt him, wanted to know if there was a way she could somehow make it right. Which was a ridiculous notion in itself. She was a lawyer, not God—and ignored the reminder of so many lawyers she knew who had difficulty with that distinction. She'd have said it out loud. Tried to make him laugh, but it wasn't the time. Especially as the thought of that other woman, *one actually carrying JD's child*, had woken a jealousy in her that she hadn't known she possessed. Had she really wished it to be her? A week ago she'd have laughed that off. Now she knew it was one more pain she'd take with her and astutely tried to avoid the questions her head was determinedly trying to make her face. Not now.

Her head slid back into the moment when he finally responded.

"Okay, I admit maybe I've been guilty of a bit of brooding." One side of those luscious lips kicked up. He caught her eyes with a quick glance, held for a moment, and then winked. Again. Slow. Sexy.

Then, just like he hadn't once more used his obvious superpower to turn her to mush, he looked away, busied himself fishing out a Brazil nut. His fingers caressed it, brought it to his mouth, crunched it with those strong teeth—and her own mouth dried. Brazil nuts—they'd never been her favorite, now she'd barely be able to look at one without triggering erotic thoughts.

Swallowing, he once more claimed her eyes. And once more held; his voice low. "But then sometimes something comes along and you realize you've been marking time in the same place for too long, and it feels good to move on."

He now had her attention completely. *Something else? Mia? Or could it be…?* She could barely even complete the thought. Had he… Could he have meant *her*?

There was no time to wonder. "Your turn." Like he'd flicked a switch, the focus had also switched. "Married? Engaged?"

Flushed from his last comment, she took a moment. Then almost by rote, the habitual dissemble for all questions about her past began to roll over her lips. Then halted. She was way past that with JD. So, just as he had before her, she assumed the same pragmatic tone.

"Like you, just one close call." She didn't add that it had broken her heart and almost broken her spirit. How it had driven home that it didn't matter how hard you worked to change your life, it would never be enough; that the life others took for granted would never be yours. "His name was

Randy—Randolph Chester Holbourne, the third."

Across from her, JD's eyes narrowed and his mouth twisted. "I dislike him already."

Unable to stop the smile that blossomed after that comment; one that had warmed her right to her toes, she continued. "Big family of bankers. And, I guess he swept me off my feet." So much so that she'd taken a chance—began to hope. Hope that she could have it all—that this was maybe the golden ticket to love and a family.

"So, what went wrong?" His mouth tightened. "And it better not be what I suspect."

Of its own accord, one shoulder lifted in response. "Lovely family; they enveloped me immediately. We got engaged, and because of who they were, that was newsworthy." Her gaze drifted away as the memories flooded back. "I was worried that my past might come out, and I didn't want it to be a shock so I told him—told Randy." She could still see his face, see the disgust in his eyes—it was a judgment she would never forget, and that expression solidified all her fears.

"He broke the engagement?" The venom in JD's voice was enough to convey his reaction. The blazing eyes, rigidly held shoulders, and the vein pulsing at his temple were just icing on the cake. And Evie wanted to throw herself across at him, and hold him. She didn't want to see him upset for her, but damn it felt nice.

"Oh, he was a gentleman about it." And yes, the brittle

laugh that slipped out may have negated that fact. "He suggested we call it off and never speak again; promised, quite benevolently in his opinion, not to tell his parents. There was one brief—distraught—phone call from his mother, bless her. I believe they think I was the one to break the engagement."

"Bastard."

She leaned across the table to him. "It's okay, JD. It could never have worked. Old news." She held out both hands, palms heavenward. "If you want the truth, I missed his parents more than I missed Randy! Ha!"

"Do you think they would have cared about your past?"

"Who knows? But Randy did, and that was what mattered. The shame of it ever coming out that his fiancée was a bastard, that his future mother-in-law was an alcoholic druggie—was apparently too much." She shrugged. "It didn't fit the narrative he'd spun."

And her world was filled with Randys. Those for whom she would never be good enough. Proof, although she hadn't really needed it, that it was her destiny to forever not fit.

He squeezed her hand, his anger still there, right under the surface. "You're really okay?"

Was there an answer to that? "Sure!" She picked up her glass. "Let's drink to those lucky escapes! Toast our good fortune."

His eyes searched her face before he drained what was left in his own glass. "I've got a better idea." Standing, he reached for her hand again, drawing her to him. "Follow me."

Unless she pulled away from him completely, she had no choice as, hands still clasped, he led her toward the far corner of the room, past a couple huddled close in the low lighting, dancing to a song just coming to an end. Right to the jukebox.

Panic arrived, fast and furious. "JD, I don't really—I can't…"

Her words were drowned by the music he'd chosen, her fear drowned by all the other burgeoning emotions she saw in his eyes.

Sultry and sexy, the opening notes of Spandeau Ballet's *True*, swirled around them, melting her disquiet, *melting her*. "I love this…"

His arms encircled her, pulled her in close. "Me too." The words were whispered against her temple. He lifted one of her arms to his shoulder, and cradled the hand of the other against his heart.

Even with nothing more than a whisper between them, he pulled her even closer—and she didn't stop him. Couldn't have stopped him. Didn't *want* to stop him.

For this moment, her world was perfect. In the arms of the man she loved; one she'd soon walk away from.

Agony and ecstasy.

Chapter Eleven

Her emotions were in turmoil, her body still throbbing with need even though it had been an hour since he'd held her against his own. Hard muscles had pressed so gently, yet so thoroughly, against her—her body answering by molding itself pliantly to their contours. Wordless promises whispered. Promises she would, for once, not deny herself.

Now, standing looking down at the sleeping baby, it felt almost wrong to be reliving every second of that dance, and yet there was no way she could turn off those memories, those images—those feelings that tingled and made her alive, so aware of her own body, so aware of his.

Somehow, they'd managed to remember their responsibilities, to peel away from each other and find their way back to the ranch. This time it was Evie who'd claimed dibs on checking on Mia, leaving JD to suffer under Nan's amused scrutiny, and to see her off.

She knew the exact moment he rejoined her, standing beside her in the barely lit room. She hadn't had to turn; she sensed him—her body recognized him. Recognized the arm that slipped around her, pulling her to him as they both gazed at the precious bundle that had brought them together. Welcomed the slight pressure that turned her to him. Gentle at first, tightening as her arms slid up around his neck and pulled him to her.

Thrilled, she pressed closer, stretched up to meet him, marveling at the powerful length of him, burning with a need she hadn't known was possible.

His muffled groan was all she heard as he scooped her up, her own surprised cry swallowed into his shoulder. Her breasts burgeoned, seeming to reach to him, and her breath caught when they were once more crushed against him. *Hurts so good.*

In three strides they were in the corridor. His arms released her to lift her face to his, her eyes to his—to the raw need calling to her. Her knees crumpled but he caught her, held her, dared her…

Flint and tinder. Together they created fire—hot, raging, tongues of fire that licked around them as they jumped in and out of the flames. It's what they'd been doing since they'd met—jumping in and out of that flame—testing, retreating; teasing, submitting, dismissing.

But now…

He didn't need words; she knew what he was asking. "Yes."

It was all he needed.

Had her feet moved or had she floated? Suddenly there

was a wall, hard at her back, but oh my, he was harder at her front. Instinctively her hands moved to rest against that chest, felt his heartbeat under her palm; a heartbeat that echoed the rapid tattoo of her own—and that empowered her, made her bold, fearless.

Reckless.

She didn't do reckless. Ever. It should have terrified her.

It didn't. It was the opposite, liberating, like she was a new woman—the woman she wanted to be.

Her eyes never left his mouth, watching it again move closer. Those lips, so full and luscious, so full of promise. A promise she knew they would deliver. Would her heart survive? Would it explode? They'd kissed before, yet this first touch of his lips on hers was like igniting that dry tinder—hot, fast airborne sparks and all consuming. And so tender.

Lips that coaxed, and persuaded, so soft and yet so firm, asking so much of her. Could he even get any closer? Oh, he could... They were one; molded to each other, joined. Curves against muscle. Every part of her throbbed, her heartbeat crashing loudly in her ears.

He was magnificent. She wanted to tell him, to... Suddenly she pulled back. Her breath ragged, her voice broken. "Wait, I can't have sex with you and call you JD! Your name? What's your name?"

"Judson. Judson Daniel." He hauled in air. "Judd. But, honey, if you're thinking about that, I'm not doing this right."

He dragged her back in, swallowing his own name on her whispered sigh. His lips once more on hers. Until *he* pulled back, panting heavily, "Just checking—you're sure about the sex?"

Her words came on broken gasps, "After four days of foreplay. You bet." She grabbed his face and pulled it back to her.

This time his lips barely left hers; his hands tangled in her hair. "You call *that* foreplay? Oh sweetheart, have we got a lot to explore."

She slid her mouth sideways, just enough to nibble at the corner of his mouth, teasing the sensitive junction with the tip of her tongue. *When had she become so brave? Bold?* On his snatched intake of air she said, "I so love exploring…"

"Four days, huh?"

The typical male pride in his rasped words thrilled her. She deepened the kiss, then, "Uh huh. You had me at *that baby is not mine.*"

Through her half-closed lashes she saw his eyes suddenly dart heavenward. "Huh?"

"You were so sure. I figured you weren't a player." She paused, imbibed once more at the well of goodness that was his lips. "Are you?"

He found her breast—*when had her shirt unbuttoned*—teasing the already erect nipple and all the air left her body on a squeal of pleasure.

"Ever?" His lips found her throat, she shuddered at his

touch and dragged in desperately needed oxygen. "Or now?"

Did she even care at that point? The lawyer in her spoke up: Yes, she should care. But what the hell... Again, he stroked her erect nipple, again her breathless response was delivered in broken spurts. "I kind... of only care... about now."

She dared to rub her hand up the stretched rough denim that encased his erection and his whole body stiffened; his words strangled. "M-my—oh sweet... r-recent history?"

"No," she ground out between gasps. "What you're going to do to me now!"

Oh God, they were really going to do this.

Once more she was scooped up into his arms, and once more they were moving. Her hands tangled in his hair, pulled him closer. "Oh—baby monitor!"

"Got it," he answered, his response breathy, rasping, teasing all the sensitive spots along her throat. "In my pocket."

Her eyes flicked open. "Oh, I thought that was—"

His chuckle was huffed. "It was. Monitor's in my back pocket." His lips curled into a smile she felt growing across the soft skin below her ear. "You thought *that* could have been the monitor?"

"Down boy." It was her own laughter, hushed so as not to disturb Mia, that carried them into his bedroom. "Your ego is way too healthy to need that kind of testimony."

"But you *did*, right?"

There was only one way to move forward and Evie took

it; sliding her lips once more against his, teasing and opening to him, feeling her whole body soften for him, readying itself as he lowered her onto his bed.

※

JD PACED. ON a rug a mere two feet away, Mia lay on her tummy, happily oblivious to the dark mood that had engulfed her uncle. He'd pulled on yesterday's jeans, so as to diminish the risk of waking Evie, grabbed a shirt that now still hung open, and hightailed it downstairs.

Happily, he'd remembered the monitor and was able to grab Mia when her jabbered babbling cooed its way across to him. Diaper changed and bottle done, he'd suddenly found himself unable to keep still.

His eyes lifted skyward, and despite his anger his body tightened as he imagined Evie in his bed; remembered the most amazing experience of his life; one that had kept him awake even after she'd dozed—looking at her, desperate to hold the moment.

Evie was used to early mornings, but after getting almost no sleep he hoped she stayed and got some rest, cursing the phone in his hand that had robbed him of extra time cuddled into that soft body. Extra time to show her how special she was in his eyes; convey to her what he feared mere words wouldn't.

Mia sneezed, and frowning he quickly bundled her up into his arms, wiping away her drool with a tissue—his thoughts immediately back on the text from Leo. Three words. Curt and clear. JD didn't have to read them again to feel the anger surging anew.

"*Cancel DNA test.*"

Leo was denying his own child? Walking away from this innocent baby? This precious gift? Had the guy completely lost his mind? Forgotten his upbringing?

JD couldn't pinpoint the exact moment—*maybe it was when Mia had first smiled at him, or maybe that first moment he'd realized she was a Halligan*—but he'd known from that point that he'd ensure Mia was part of her family—even, he'd mused at the time, if that meant adopting her himself.

It had only been a halfhearted thought because he'd been sure Leo would step up. Now as he held the other man's daughter, her head snuggled into his shoulder, he wondered if he knew his brother at all. One thing was certain. Actually, two things. First, Mia would be his, safe, protected and loved. And second, his respect for his brother was dead.

With no concern for time differences, JD punched out one of the numbers he'd been trying to reach every day since this whole thing had begun, surprised when this time someone answered. Shifting Mia into a slightly more comfortable position, did nothing to curb his irritation. "Where in the he—*heck* is he, Joe? What's going on?"

Joe didn't immediately respond, and JD imagined the old guy chewing on his *baccy*, as he processed. He was a crony of their dad, a seasoned rodeo guy, who'd never managed to make a life outside, but was also one of the most respected men on the circuit. JD knew from experience he'd be keeping Leo in his sights, so if anyone knew anything, it'd be Joe, which only made the fact he'd also been avoiding their calls all the more mysterious.

"He's not here, JD. He got on a plane a day or so ago."

Joe's answer confirmed he had Leo's ear, and a part of JD, as always, was glad for his brother but another part was steaming over the fact that Joe hadn't pulled rank and sent Leo packing.

"Is he coming home? He's needed here and this ridiculous game of hide-and-seek is getting real old. We're over it and we need to get his butt here pronto."

"Let him be, JD." The words were delivered on a growl honed through years of a diet primarily of whiskey and tobacco. "He's hurtin' real bad. He'll get hisself home, but just let up on him a bit. It ain't easy. Give the boy time to do what he's got to do." There was another pause before the older man added, "I'm askin' this as a favor, both to me and your brother, and I'm hopin' you'll respect that."

They ended the call on that note. JD rocked his head back on his shoulders, his eyes searching the ceiling for clarity. Finding none, he tossed the phone onto a nearby sofa. Frustration warred with logic. He trusted Joe—and if he was being fair, he trusted his brother, too. Or at least he had. Until now.

Still, Joe seemed sure that Leo was on his way home, but

he hadn't clarified whether it was a direct journey. Was Joe right? Did Leo need space? The upside of accepting that suggestion meant more time with Evie…

In the end, it was that thought that solidified his decision. He'd give Leo space; tell Jack to back off for a few days, but that didn't mean Leo was being granted any more leeway, and once he arrived back home, his brother would have no doubts about the depths of his disappointment.

The curt message he'd received earlier still rankled. He and his brothers hadn't always seen eye to eye, but JD had never faced a situation before where he didn't still respect them.

That message changed all that…

🍎

"HI… ARE YOU okay?" He only felt the soft hand against his arm after he'd heard her words. And only saw the faint hurt in her eyes after he'd allowed himself to look into that beautiful face.

Pulling her close with his free arm, he momentarily closed his eyes. There *was* good in the world—and he was holding it under his arm. "Yeah, I'm fine. We're fine. Princess here was a bit sneezy but maybe something tickled her nose because she doesn't have a fever."

When Evie again looked up, the hurt was gone and once more that luminescent gaze seemed to seep right into him; warming him. Stretching up on tiptoes she brushed her lips against his. "You're a good uncle. Thank you for allowing me to rest. Although I was a bit sad to wake and find you gone."

He kissed the top of her head. "Phone call."

"Oh? Everything alright?"

He looked down into that upturned face. She was glowing. Literally glowing. No frown lines creased her forehead, and he thought she looked the most relaxed she'd looked since arriving. And he couldn't take this moment away from her. Not now. Not yet. It could wait. "Yeah… Just business. I'll sort it later."

He bent to place Mia on the rug. "But right now, I'm treating you to breakfast. The best breakfast I can muster…" He paused and once more looked at her, unable to control the hoarseness of his voice when he began to speak. "The best breakfast I can create for the most beautiful woman in the world."

Her mouth opened but no words emerged. Instead, her eyes filled, and he watched her try to swallow them back. "I…"

What passed as a growl cleared the sudden lump forming in his own throat, and he planted a quick kiss on those delectable lips, ignoring his body's plea for more. "Go play with Mia. This won't take long."

"JD!" He'd taken barely three steps when her voice stopped him. Alarmed he turned to her, confused by the look of wonder in her eyes. "Mia. Look at her!"

He did, and everything surged inside him and out. Excitement bubbled through his chest, his grin impossible to contain. "She's sitting up by herself?" His whoop reached the rafters.

"I know!" When he turned back to Evie, it was hard to look away. Eyes sparkling, her hands in the prayer position, pressed against those luscious lips, ripe and swollen after their night together, lips now spread in a smile that radiated—lit the room.

Her laughter joined his and he joined her joyous clapping before she dropped to her knees, her golden-toned legs and thighs exposed as she leaned forward. He tried not to look but really?

Mere human...

Smooth, naked and alluring—all under the white T-shirt she'd obviously found in his room. His T-shirt.

"Clever girl!" Evie's praise was acknowledged with a cheeky squeal, and he dragged his eyes back to the baby.

JD hunkered down beside Evie, so close their shoulders touched, closer even after he'd wrapped an arm around her to hold her near—and focused on Mia. "What are the odds,' he murmured, "that one man should have the most beautiful woman and the smartest baby both with him at the same time? You've got one very lucky uncle, little one."

And his voice cracked a little bit over the word uncle.

Breakfast pushed to the backburner for the moment, they simply continued to fuss over baby Mia; JD finally remembering his phone so they could get some shots for

Hope. And, he knew, for himself. *For them.* Memories.

Captured by the adults' excitement, Mia showed off all her tricks for her adoring audience, rolling over and pushing herself up to a seated position, her chubby arms supporting her. When she began to tire, Evie moved to sit behind her, support her. And JD moved to sit so he supported Evie.

"You'd think we were her parents," he whispered, watching the interplay between the woman and her charge.

"This must be exactly what it feels like," she responded. "The pride—the relief that they've achieved a milestone without obstacles, the joy of witnessing such a huge step. Do you think she even knows she's achieved something so special?"

"I don't know, but I'm wondering how we'll be when she starts crawling, or when she takes her first step, if we're this excited about her sitting up by herself." As soon as the words were out he wished them back, didn't have to wonder if it would kill the mood. It was right there in her face—the reminder she wouldn't be there to share those future milestones.

Unhappy with himself was an understatement, but in truth, he'd hardly been thinking straight since he'd awakened to that damned text message. Still, maybe it hadn't been the disaster he'd first thought. *Fate, remember?* Instead, maybe it provided the opening to address something he'd been thinking about all night long. And probably even before that if he counted his dreams which had been on the job way before his conscious mind.

Curling an arm around her, he shifted slightly to be better able to see her face. Finding the right words proved a bit harder, but eventually he whispered, "It doesn't have to be that way. You can still share those moments."

She twisted, to look straight at him. "What are you saying?"

Mouth suddenly dry, he still pressed on. "Stay here. With me. Be part of Mia's life."

Her eyes searched his face, assessing, processing. "And give up my work?"

"I'm just saying—*suggesting, asking*—that you stay here with us. With this family."

Her mouth opened. Floundered.

Flicking a quick kiss right there against that open mouth, he continued. "We seem to have this thing goin' on, and it's a good thing. A damned good thing. A thing like I've never experienced before. I don't know how it's affected you…?" She nodded her agreement and he dropped another kiss. "What I'm not sure about is if you realize how rare this is? How rare this thing is."

He watched her inhale. Deep and slow.

"And you'd be here for Mia," he continued, "someone to support Hope because I'm hoping at some stage she'd be able to come out here. Live here." It was a new thought but he liked it; knew that if Hope got well, he'd make sure of it. Just as he'd make sure Mia was cared for after…

Evie's wide-eyed unblinking gaze, stared steadily back at him. Then it was gone hidden under long, dark lashes that swept over her cheek. His breath held, and he felt his heartbeat right through his body, pulsing, picking up speed. What was she thinking?

When she lifted her eyes, they were clouded. "It's the dream, isn't it? Hope to recover. Us to have this life…" Her shrug came with a halfhearted laugh. "But I'm sorry, JD. I don't know. There's so much in what you said that I want to grab and run with it. Grab and hold it close and yell, *mine!* But I just—"

He expelled the breath he was holding on a rush of gratitude. It hadn't been a *no*, right? And as long as she didn't know about Leo's decision, he had time to convince her. Time to show her that he loved her; that he, unlike all the others in her life, wouldn't be walking away.

❦

EVIE LET THE warm water wash down over her body, marveling that she looked just the same as she had yesterday. Yet, she'd never again be that girl of yesterday. JD's touch had changed her, awakened her—rather like the prince's kiss had awakened Sleeping Beauty. She'd never considered herself to be a passionate person—in her experience passion was on a par with recklessness. Recklessness led to bad decisions.

Last night had changed that perception of herself. Last

night she learned how much of herself she'd held tight, how afraid she'd been to let go—to enjoy the moment. Afraid to choose the unknown path.

Last night had been reckless.

And wonderful and stupendous and amazing and all the other superlatives. Every single one of them. JD had not only dared her, he'd encouraged her, led her, guided her—and the moment she realized he had become the follower was so very powerful. And so very humbling.

It wasn't only about sex, although that was something else she'd totally changed her perspective of. No, it was about togetherness; of finally feeling complete—like finally finding that piece of yourself you hadn't even realized was missing. A piece she'd leave behind when she left here.

If, a little voice whispered. *If* you leave here.

Tears joined the water sluicing over her. How could she possibly leave here, leave JD? Yet how could she possibly stay?

He was the proverbial path unknown. Sure, she knew how wonderful he was, how kind and caring, how dedicated, how funny he was—how he made her laugh and be silly. That thought pulled her up short. Had she been gradually letting go since she first met him? Had last night simply been the dawning of the inevitable? That it was meant to be? But how can anybody be sure?

Confusion clouded all rational thought, and spurred doubt that curled and snaked through her. Her career was her security; walking away from the firm would be akin to stepping off a plane without a parachute.

But then again, hadn't she just been questioning her purpose? Questioning whether she could be using her law degree to really make a difference instead of making rich fat cats richer? How? How would she accomplish that?

She closed her eyes and again those whispered words replayed in her head; words she hadn't been able to vanquish. *Stay here. With me.*

Frustration warred with doubt. This was the very reason she didn't do relationships. And what of JD? If she stayed but somehow continued to work, how would that sit with him? She wasn't a fool. No matter how he argued to the contrary, JD was possibly still festering after his disastrous relationship with a city business woman. When this magnetic attraction between them began to pall, would her career become an issue?

She'd found no answers by the time she stepped out and dried herself on one of the soft blue towels JD had provided. Even choosing an outfit was causing confusion, or at least a top to go with her jeans. Eventually she just grabbed the first shirt off the pile and which coincidentally was the same aqua shade as her eyes. It wasn't a shirt so much as a stretchy cotton, scooped-neck, fitted sweater that hugged every curve and not like anything she'd ever worn before—and for that reason probably the most suited to her present mood.

And still confused when she finally returned downstairs

to a breakfast for a king. Surely no queen, conscious of her figure, would be able to tackle the mountain of food JD was transporting to the table—though if she needed confirmation of her clothing choice, she didn't have to search further than the expression in JD's eyes as they roved down over her, narrowing on the now-peaked nipples evident where the top hugged her breasts.

Yes, he aroused her. He knew that, so she refused to show any discomfit and straightened her shoulders as she first fussed with Mia, now sitting up in her high chair, before turning her attention fully to the food.

A mouthwatering fluffy omelet, sausage, fried tomato, hash browns, and just now coming out of the oven, what looked like cinnamon rolls.

Eyes wide she stood and surveyed it all. "Most people," she began, "don't eat their day's three meals in one sitting."

One eyebrow rose. At the return of their cheeky banter? If so, he appreciated it if the twitch of his mouth was any indication. "*Most people* didn't spend the night working up an appetite." His voice dropped low. "Just the very fortunate ones."

After that night spent together, she didn't think he'd have the power to make her blush, but there, he just went and did it. Taking a seat and pretending her face wasn't on fire she pursed her lips. "Most people know it's not polite to brag."

"That so? Well darlin, *most* people who'd experienced

what I did last night would want to shout it from the mountain top."

Mia agreed. Or maybe she was merely expressing her enjoyment of the buttered crust she'd now managed to spread right across her face and up into her hair to mingle with the cereal already smeared there.

"See?" JD said on a deep chuckle. "Even she's on my side. At least with the breakfast part. And she's right—we need to eat up because there's a whole day of adventure waiting right outside that door."

Of course he finished with a wink. Slow and sexy. And all for her.

She tried to steady her breathing. Did he realize how her body shimmied every time that whiskey voice rumbled over her? How even just his laugh made her come alive? Made her want to reach out and touch him? Be near him?

The bigger question was whether she wanted him to know.

She looked up from the plate he'd filled for her to find his eyes on her, watching her. Maybe he already knew too much…

❦

JD HAD BEEN true to his word. As she discovered over the following three days, adventure had indeed awaited just outside the door. In fact, a whole lifetime of it, if she chose to take it.

She'd sat atop Sugar, been led around the corral, her confidence growing each day, a bond growing between her and the horse, and she'd loved every moment. From JD's hands about her waist as he'd helped her mount and alight, to his gentle encouragement, his patient guidance to the soul-jarring kisses that were her reward.

With each meal he'd encouraged her to help prepare, praising her successes, and laughing with her over her failures, and never once in judgment. They'd picnicked, and barbequed, fussed over the animals, learned about ranch life—and in the evening they'd slow-danced with a sleepy baby snuggled between them.

All of this, if she left, would remain in her heart, in her head, tattooed on her soul. But it was the nights, those glorious nights filled with passion: nights spent in his arms where they took and they gave, nights of building and release, of being sated but not quite… Because it seemed it would never be enough; she could never get enough of him. She would never be done; she would want him forever.

He hadn't asked her about staying since that day, but she knew the question hadn't been rescinded—still there—the one cloud in an otherwise brilliant blue sky.

Still, a decision had to be made one way or the other. With Leo still unable to be contacted, it was becoming more obvious to her that he wasn't interested in being a father to Mia. And her job wouldn't sit there indefinitely. Despite her bosses' proclamation regarding her time off, barely veiled queries about her return date had already appeared.

She'd tried valiantly to weigh it all, and every time the scales had tipped heavily on remaining here in Montana with JD. She loved him. Of course, it was what she wanted, but was she brave enough to take that chance?

Some of her decision had been influenced by Mia. Mia's trust, her brave spirit, was there in the dozens of photographs they sent Hope, in the hours of video reels. Mia had complete trust, something that shamed Evie because she herself had allowed so little trust in her life.

Hope's responses had become more and more brief, and often not at all. Once when Evie had phoned, a man had answered in a low voice, advising that she was too ill to take the call; and always, her heart heavy, Evie hugged that baby even more. Not only for herself, but for her mama as well. Yes, there were lessons to be learned everywhere, even from a six-month-old baby.

Now this morning, as she readied to head downstairs to where both the man she loved and the baby she adored waited, she checked herself in the mirror, happy enough with the jeans and a lemon-colored shirt. But even happier about something else.

Today she would tell JD she needed to go into town. Go to buy new clothes because if she was really staying here, she at least needed her own wardrobe.

And she couldn't wait to see his face.

Mia's arms stretched to her the moment she saw Evie

step off the last stair. Taking her from JD's arms, Evie nuzzled the baby's neck, loving the squeals and screeches, inhaling that precious baby smell, holding her tight against her heart—her urgency to share her decision with JD held in abeyance for just a few minutes.

Unaware Mia had ambushed Evie's moment, JD chuckled at the hijinks, reaching over to tickle Mia's tummy, causing an even more riotous response.

It was probably due to the noise they were making that they were unaware another person had entered the room—entered the house—until he spoke.

"I think I'd like you to hand over my daughter."

Chapter Twelve

*L**EO?*

The room fell silent. Even Mia stilled, staring solemnly at the man she didn't recognize but was her reason for existence.

Even if his words hadn't given him away, Evie would have recognized him. Like JD and Jack, he had that strong physique—tall and broad across the shoulders. His hair was darker, but if you bypassed the bloodshot and shadows, the eyes staring out from under his black felt hat were just as dark and just as searching.

Where they differed was that this version of the Halligan brothers was pretty battered. One arm was encased in a sling and the other leaned heavily on a walking stick.

Stunned, Evie was still trying to fathom her feelings about what Leo's return meant, when JD spoke. "What the hell took you so long?"

The tone was so sharp Mia whimpered, earning JD a glare from Evie, and even one from the babe's errant father.

Leo sighed. "Not now, JD. It's been a tough couple of days and I've come straight from the airport."

JD's chest rose, his nostrils flared. *"You've had a tough*

couple of days? Have you given a thought to what you've done? What you've put others through? What this baby's mother is going through? Wh—"

"She's gone." Leo's voice broke, and it was like the rest of him broke right along with it. His eyes filled; the shadows under them seemed to deepen. Seemingly needing that stick to hold him up. "Hope passed away two days ago."

Her gasp brought all eyes to her. *No, no, no...* She wanted to rail, to tell this man to stop saying such things but really—hadn't this been what she'd suspected? Deep down, hadn't she known in her heart? Dreaded? Hope had been growing weaker, not stronger. "How do—"

Leo cut off her question. "I was with her. Been with her these past few days. Not long enough. I should have been there when... Be-before..."

Pain tore through Evie. Overwhelming sadness was only surpassed by the anger that burned hard and fast. Anger that such a beautiful human could be struck down so mercilessly, so young—and with a lifetime of love before her with her daughter. Anger for Mia, who was deprived of her mother; one who would have loved and cherished her. Anger for herself, that she'd found the one best friend she'd had, only to lose her so quickly.

And as she watched the man before her crumple, watched his tears, heard his anguish—anger for Leo who had obviously lost someone so special.

Passing Mia quickly to a stunned JD, Evie rushed to drag

out a chair, easing Leo into it, held him against her as his tears flowed.

They made him tea, forced him to eat—even if it was only toast. Made him rest. All the time she and JD barely spoke, didn't touch, kept their distance. Leo was back, and what did that mean? What did it mean for *them*?

Later, showered, and looking slightly more in control, Leo finished his story. "Weeks back I had an accident. Not on the circuit—which was why," he added looking over at JD, "you didn't hear about it. I got messed about pretty good when I tangled with a loaded cattle truck. It got serious. Old Joe was with me and I swore him to secrecy."

Evie knew JD was worried, but she could still see the anger simmering just under the surface. "What kind of fool idea was that?"

Leo sucked in air. "Yeah, I know, but it was for Mom. They were just about to leave and I wasn't going to be the reason she canceled that trip. Joe's been riding shotgun for me for weeks, heading off any questions. We had a story concocted and nobody on the circuit questioned it." He paused. "He saw Jack's message about a baby, and someone named Hope and knew I'd want to know." His eyes lowered. "She was special. He'd heard me jabbering on about her."

"But you left her." There was still no sympathy in JD's tone.

"I begged her to come with me. Promised her I'd be back after she said she needed time to think. And I did—did go back for her—but I couldn't find her. She'd been kicked out of her crummy apartment and no one knew where she was. None of the deadbeats in her building had a clue." He swiped a hand across his face. "I had to go or miss the rodeo, but I was going to go back after Christmas and tear that city apart till I found her."

"You didn't call her?"

He shrugged. "She lost her job when she was pregnant, Evie; couldn't afford her phone for months so she had no service." He shrugged. "Of course, I only just found that out. And she couldn't get me because after *my* phone got stolen, I had to get a new number, too. Remember?"

Evie sat, feeling the weight of it all pressing down on her. They'd both failed Hope in their own way. But now there was Mia, and she'd be damned if anyone was going to fail that child. "And Mia?"

Leo looked across at JD. "She's mine. I didn't doubt it from the moment I heard Hope was the mother."

JD nodded; eyes solemn. "I'm so sorry, bro. Sorry I doubted you."

In a mirror image of his brother, Leo raised one eyebrow. "Yeah, I figured you'd got the wrong end of the stick when I got your—ahem *eloquent*—texts. But by then I had too much on my hands." He shrugged. "As soon as I heard about Hope, I discharged myself from the hospital; made my way straight to San Francisco. I knew you and Jack would take care of my little girl, but I just had to see her mama. To apologize for not trying harder to find her; to tell her I loved her and that our child would have a good life—and then I swear I was coming straight back here."

"You could have called."

Weariness rolled off Leo on heavy waves as he rocked his head back, looking across at his big brother, his eyes half concealed under leaden lids. "I kinda had a lot on my plate, and as I said, I trusted you to do what had to be done—just like I had to do what I needed to do. But yeah, maybe that was a blunder and I apologize, especially," he added, moving his gaze away from JD, "to you Evie."

Evie found her voice. "Hope would have been so at peace to know that Mia would be loved. Thank you. You, um, knew about her past?"

He nodded. "Yep. There wasn't much we didn't share that first time we met. That first, and only week we had together." The look he sent her was one of pure sympathy. "You both had it pretty rough."

It was too much. Grateful that Mia had begun to grizzle, Evie, wordlessly took her upstairs to settle her for a nap. As she rocked the baby off to sleep, so much was going around in her head. Sorrow for the loss of Hope hung heavily, even though she knew part of her was grieving for the ten-year-old Hope, now gone forever.

But, sure, there was also relief in one way that Mia would be securely taken care of, that the problem wasn't hers any longer. Furthermore, there'd be no necessary work compromises; it could continue as it had before this had happened.

Continue *what* before this happened? A voice inside her head scoffed. *What?* A lonely life populated by a couple of acquaintances who weren't even close enough to have called this week? Filled by *work* she didn't enjoy and didn't satisfy her? Kept warm by a growing bank balance?

She closed her eyes, unable to contain the tears that silently flowed, holding the baby closer, feeling her soft warmth, watching her little chest pump up and down, relishing the tiny fist that curled around her pinky.

There'd be no more of this. She'd known it would be heartbreaking, but it had always been inevitable. Starkly put, she was no longer needed. At least not to care for Mia. A tiny flag of hope soared. But JD? Did *he* need her?

A shuffling noise made her look up, frowning through the gloom of the afternoon light. Even the weather had flipped to match their mood. Leo stood in the doorway, moving slowly closer after Evie's nod.

He peered down at the baby. His baby. His eyes, even in this poor light, filled with the awe that she'd seen in JD's eyes and probably what others saw in hers. "I just wanted to see her again," he whispered. He'd held her earlier, his struggle visible. She thought she understood—she'd immediately noticed the intense likeness between mother and daughter and for him that must be even more poignant.

"She's beautiful."

He nodded. "Just like her mama." He touched Evie's

shoulder, still whispering. "Hope told me about you. Told me how you'd come to her rescue and I can't ever thank you enough. I can see Mia's been loved."

"Not only by me. JD is a fine uncle." Another rush of tears threatened and Evie pushed them back as best she could. "Will there be a... a funeral?"

His eyes squeezed shut for a moment. "The hospital chaplain was good to Hope. He and I had a private service in the chapel there, and once she... her ashes get couriered here, I'd like to have a service over at my ranch. Bury her ashes there so Mia will know where her mama is resting." Tears leaked through, forging a damp trail down his cheek. "The nurses printed some of the photos you sent. Photos of Mia. When you took Mia, Hope said she knew she was saying good-bye for the last time, and she tried to make her peace with that in the knowledge that her daughter was with you, the one person she trusted. But she never let them out of her sight; died clutching one to her chest and me holding her other hand. It was like we were all together. Thank you."

Evie made no effort to stem the tide of tears this time, glad for Mia's sake that they flowed quietly.

"And I'm sorry," he continued, "for that damned stupid message I sent JD a few days back. It must have messed you guys around." He shook his head ever so slightly. "I can see why he thought I wasn't going to step up and claim Mia, but that was never going to happen."

Evie frowned as his words rolled around in her head.

"JD's known, or thought he knew, you weren't intending on claiming Mia? For a few days?"

"Sent it Wednesday; the day they told me Hope didn't have that long." He sighed. "I should have been clearer, but my head wasn't exactly screwed on tight that day. Don't think it is yet."

She squeezed his hand, indicating she should put Mia in her bed. But after Leo had gone, selfishly she couldn't make herself move. Part of it was her reluctance to be separated from the child, all too aware of how few opportunities to do this were left.

But part of it was also what she had just learned. JD had believed Leo wasn't going to take Mia, *before* he'd asked her to stay? Was that significant? Had it really merely been about raising Mia?

Images of JD sprang to mind way too easily. Now, he'd too, been released from the responsibility of raising a child alone, would that rescind his invitation? And how would that play out in the future if she came to visit Mia?

Would she see him? *Could* she see him? Suffer the torture of perhaps seeing him with a wife, family?

It had been a cruel joke, really. Open door Number One and see your dream life. A warm family home. A gorgeous child. And a man who takes your breath away, who makes your heart beat so hard, who makes your knees weak—all because he smiled at you.

A man who would have your back.

A man who made you yearn for the impossible…

In the end Evie didn't put Mia in her crib, she simply held her, knowing it wasn't the best decision. But she needed it.

And it saved her from having to face JD; saved her from the pain of seeing rejection in his eyes. Allowed her to hold on to hope, to her dream, for a little bit longer.

Evie couldn't hide forever though. Dinner was a quiet affair, and as though Mia picked up the vibe, she pulled on her cranky pants, putting on a full-blown show for her visibly disconcerted father.

By the time the baby was bathed, fed and settled, it had grown late. She and JD had still barely exchanged a word, so she readied for bed, intending to stay in her room and wait for him there.

But that was the thing. He didn't come.

In the early hours she'd given up expecting him, given up hoping he'd come to her and gave over to clearly examining the situation and mentally laying out her options. She'd cried and dozed, cried and dozed. Cursed herself for being every kind of fool; for daring to swim out of her lane.

Recalibrated.

It was clear JD had had a change of heart. She didn't fully blame him. He'd been as blindsided by this whole episode in their lives as she had; probably just as caught up in the fantasy.

Except now there was no fantasy. Only real life.

Well, she'd had enough of real life.

Most of all, she was tired of people who wouldn't go the distance. In the past she'd been the one left behind. Maybe this was the first step of her new life, but this time she'd be the one to do the leaving.

It wouldn't cure her broken heart. It wouldn't help her get over him. And it wouldn't stop her wishing that he loved her back.

But there'd be at least some element of satisfaction. Wouldn't there? And it would save another awkward breakup scene and all the *it wasn't you* comments that were bound to be thrown around. *That,* she truly couldn't handle. Not today and not tomorrow.

Packing took no time, after all she only originally intended to stay a couple of days—and this time she wasn't packing for a baby. All of Mia's things would stay.

Evie glanced down at the sleeping child. Her little face seemed to glow, even in the pre-dawn gloom. Those rosebud lips making that odd little sucking movement as she slept. Funny how she did that…

She thought back to those first moments of having Mia. Had it only been days ago? Not months? Just days. But in that time, she learned the baby's rhythms, her whims and quirks. She wanted to think that Mia had stolen her heart, but the truth was she'd given it freely.

Mia had taught her so much. Taught her so much about herself, forced her to open her heart, forced her to examine her life—to stop pretending she had all she needed. To stop living in fear.

Had Mia taught her to love?

Or was it that Mia had prepared her for love? Prepared her to dare hope for it. Choking back a sob, she picked up a baby blanket from the end of the crib, lifted it to her face, smelled that clean sweet baby scent. And tucked it into the top of her suitcase. There were plenty of others; JD wouldn't even know it was gone.

And probably in a few days he wouldn't even realize *she* was gone. His busy life would resume, and he had a brother to help recover as well as a baby to care for.

Tears were falling in earnest now, and she feared she'd wake Mia, but still she had to lean down to press one more feather-light kiss on the baby's brow. "Bye-bye, sweet angel," she whispered. "Have a wonderful life. Remember your daddy and uncles love you so much, and your mama will always be looking down on you. Watching you, keeping you safe." She tried to swallow; sniffed. "And though you'll probably never know it, I will always love you."

And she knew it was just gas, maybe a baby dream, but Mia smiled. The sweetest, cutest, sleepy smile, one that Evie chose to believe was meant for her. And her heart clutched.

No matter how much it hurt her heart, Evie knew it was the truth—Mia would never know she loved her. It was one of the decisions she'd made through the night. A clean break—that was what they all needed. She knew she couldn't return, couldn't risk seeing JD. Couldn't continue to put herself through that torture.

Though as she quietly made her way through the silent house, out to the rental car whose lease she'd thankfully extended, she acknowledged that while returning would be torture, it surely couldn't hurt as much as this moment; hurt as much as leaving…Leaving the one place in her life that felt like home, the one place she'd found love. Well, at least found *how* to love.

Her chest was so tight; ached so much it hurt to haul in air. Still, just like breathing was an instinctive repetitive action, she, too, would endure. She'd survive. She'd survived on her own for most of her thirty-one years; having no one but herself to rely on more often than not. She could do it again.

OF ALL THE mornings for there to be fog. Still, without that fog, Evie would probably already be on her way to San Francisco, so he'd be better making his peace with it. That thought lasted about thirty seconds. Again JD squinted through the windscreen, thumped the dash, needing to do something to expel some of the pent-up frustration that had continued to build since the first moment he'd realized she'd gone.

It hadn't been his first response.

He replayed every moment of that morning, all going

around in his head, whiling away the miles.

Shock, fear, anger—they'd all played a part, each taking the lead at various stages through the questions, self-recriminations, blame and angst. But nothing had surpassed the overwhelming sense of emptiness, aloneness. How could one small woman leave a huge rambling house and make it feel empty and cold?

Three people remained and yet everywhere he looked he just found empty spaces—the biggest and most painful being the one inside him.

Why would she leave like that? Without a word? He'd hardly slept a wink, missing her by his side, trying to decipher everything in his head—wondering if she'd come to him.

Being unsure was something new to him—and he didn't like it. Even when he'd learned the truth about Samantha, he hadn't prevaricated. He'd known what had to happen; carried it through. This time was different. This was about Evie.

It had taken falling in love with Evie to understand he'd never really loved Samantha. And it was that love, that fear of losing her at the root of all this uncertainty. There was no humor in the fact that he'd suddenly visualized himself like one of those cartoons with an angel on one shoulder and a devil on the other.

And dammit, the devil's voice was louder. He'd fought for logic—Leo would take Mia, he'd be her father, her caregiver. Not him. And that was a good thing; she'd be where she belonged.

The devil had once more intervened. *But without that child in his life, would he be enough for Evie?* He hadn't kidded himself Mia was part of the deal. He'd taken advantage of that and he wasn't proud, but he'd been desperate—after all, even though he now knew he hadn't loved Samantha, it didn't change the fact that he hadn't been enough for *her*, had he?

Gritty-eyed and sleep-deprived he'd finally found sense. Decided to go to her, even though it was only just past dawn, he'd carry her back to his bed, to where she should have been, and he'd show her, tell her, how much he wanted her to stay.

He'd gone to her, but her bed had been empty. Neatly made. All her belongings gone. Only the faint scent of her perfume evidence that she'd ever been there.

Leo, dragged from his bed, interrogated, had watched quietly as JD'd stomped about the family room, finally voicing an opinion when JD had paused to draw breath. "Go after her."

He'd whirled to face his brother. "But what if she—" He hadn't even been able to say the words—*doesn't want me?*

"And you're prepared to sit on your ass and wonder about that for the rest of your life? Thought you had more in you, brother."

JD had straightened, head tilted slightly back, staring

down at his brother through narrowed eyes, half-lowered lashes.

Leo sighed, long slow and one of the saddest sounds JD had ever heard. "Don't be an idiot, JD. If you love her, and from the way she was mooning at you yesterday, I got a pretty fair notion she loves you back—then don't let her go. Don't risk losing that. Look at me..." He swallowed, struggled for a moment. "I lost my chance. And I'd give heaven and earth to be in your shoes right now—to have the opportunity to make it right again. To have Hope back with me, to be given one more chance."

JD heard his brother's pain, hurt for him, grateful they could talk so openly. "Evie's different, Leo. Determined. Her career—"

"So?" Leo shrugged. "Make it work." His own eyes narrowed. "JD? She's not Samantha. That was one selfish woman, out for herself first and everyone else came a poor second. You included."

He let that hang. Silent while JD quietly cursed.

"And you know," Leo continued, "I agree with you that Evie's different. For starters she's as different from Samantha as night is to day. Proof? You and I know exactly what Evie did, what she risked. Not many would do that. That's one special lady, one with her heart in the right place. She brought Mia here to take her rightful place with our family, JD, and it seems to me that there's another space that needs filling. The one by your side. But only if you've got the guts to go after her."

"*Guts?*" Surely this smart-assed little brother knew he was playing with fire? "You know if you weren't all banged up already, I'd be taking my best shot right now."

Leo shrugged. "Go for it anyway. It won't change anything. I'll still be right and you know it."

JD flopped into the chair beside his brother. They hadn't scuffled since they were teenagers and both knew they weren't going to start up again now. It wasn't who they were. Besides, everything Leo said had been correct. He hadn't even needed the reminder. It was what had been going around in his head all night. Still, it hadn't hurt to hear it again, to play devil's advocate and hear his own logic sprayed back at him.

"So?" Leo said. "What are you waiting for?"

"How about for you to grow another arm so I can safely leave you with your daughter!"

"No need for that. I'm here and quite capable of taking care of an invalid and a baby."

They both turned to the new voice, watching as Nan divested herself of bags and boxes, some of which JD knew would contain food. "Wha—"

She ignored him, directing her words to Leo. "I came as soon as I got your message." Striding forward she dropped a kiss on his head. "Welcome home darlin', though I'm mighty sorry to hear your news." To JD she simply said, "You still here?"

JD shook his head. "Pretty sure of yourself, little brother."

Leo shrugged in reply. "You were going after her. I refuse to have a stupid brother. Bad for the Halligan brand." He glanced at the clock. "And I figure if you leave now, you'll make it. I checked the flights. Heavy fog. First flight out of Bozeman to San Francisco is in just under three hours. I reckon she'll be needing a bit of a distraction by now. You could provide it."

He hoped he could provide more than that. A distraction was momentary. He wanted forever.

The fog was starting to lift when he reached the airport, but the backed-up flights meant the parking lot was even more full than usual which, in turn, meant his patience level was even lower than usual. He flicked a glance at the clock on the dash. The trip had been slow, in half an hour they'd be calling to board passengers.

He'd just about given up hope of getting to her in time when a space miraculously opened up, allowing him to park and sprint across to the correct terminal. Luck stayed with him—especially in the form of a forward-thinking brother. Leo had sent him a ticket via text, one that would allow him to get right to the departure gates. Of course, if this quest worked, Leo would always take the credit.

And if it didn't work?

JD couldn't—*wouldn't*—let himself think about the alternative.

He knew the airport layout well, so could move around the crowds of people quickly, his long legs eating up the distance, sure he could find her gate number without too much effort—all the while listening to the tinny announcements calling flight numbers and destinations.

He'd heard the call for San Francisco three times already, hope still alive in a heart working overtime. He had to find her. He would not lose her. And if she didn't want him? Well, he'd know.

She had feelings for him, that much he knew. He'd had enough experience with women to know a person couldn't make love like she had, given so much of herself unless it truly mattered. What he didn't know was whether she knew that.

The final call was being announced as he was nearing the gate, his eyes quickly surveying the remaining travelers, stragglers, wondering if she was already on board. Most of the waiting-area seats were empty, possibly only those there to say good-bye, remained.

He was striding toward the final check-through, to the officious looking woman checking tickets—his head screeching that as long as that plane was still on the tarmac, he had a chance. And if it failed? If he missed her? He'd get on the next flight. Follow her.

It was a trick of light that saved him.

He'd been searching as he strode along, twisting from right to left, when something stopped him; pulled him up short. The gleam off that golden hair. He'd seen it at the ranch, the way the light played with the strands that, at times, glistened like real gold.

She sat alone in a row of attached seats anchored to a wall behind, her head bowed. Her carry-on at her feet. And even without seeing her face, he knew she was upset and his chest tightened.

Moving through the rows slowly, he slid quietly into the seat beside her, removed his hat, swiped a hand through his hair. She, however, didn't move, didn't lift her head.

His heart felt overfull just at the sight of her, like it might burst and he took a moment to slow his breathing, control the urge to haul her into his arms and kiss her senseless.

Still she seemed oblivious; lost in her own world. Was she thinking about him? *About them?* He leaned slightly her way, using the closeness to gently shoulder-bump her. "*Most people*," he began on a voice broken and choked with emotion, "say good-bye when they leave."

Her head lifted, but she didn't turn his way, allowing him to see the fat tears balancing precariously on those long dark lashes. To watch them fall when she blinked, to run in smooth rivers down her face, still so beautiful despite being flushed and swollen from crying.

Pushing back into the seat he leaned his head against the wall, stared straight ahead. It killed him to watch her like this and his arms ached to hold her, console her, but she was giving him nothing.

Until, "*Most people* let that person be; let them go with dignity." Her voice tore at him; so thin and reedy.

He pulled in air. Steadied himself. The flight attendant was looking their way, the clock was ticking. This was his shot.

"Then *most* people aren't in love with the one who left."

The fingers that had been shredding a tissue, stilled. She'd heard.

"Most people don't fall in love in a week."

"Most people would if they were given the right opportunity. Anyway, who says it took a whole week? To use your analogy, you had me at the moment you stood before me clutching my sleeping niece, dead on your feet, yet so determined to make me face what you thought were my responsibilities. You've been in my head, my dreams—and in my heart since that moment."

She shuffled in her seat. Crossed her legs. Wearing that pearl gray skirt…

He didn't gape. In truth he could look at her all day long and never tire of the view, but her physical beauty was just one part of her, one part of the whole woman he'd come to love. Appreciated, yet knowing it was just one of the cherries on the most luscious bowl of ice cream he'd ever been presented. The skirt was sexy whether she knew it or not, but to him she'd be sexy in sackcloth.

She'd begun speaking again and he tuned back in. "Most

people confuse sex with love."

"*Great sex*," he corrected, side-eyeing her, noting the slightest twitch of her lips. "Another gem from psych 101?"

"Uh-huh. *Ask Agatha."*

His head rocked back, and he was unable to pull back the small grin. *She'd listened?* The trite admission, and the passing seconds, gave him the impetus to move forward. He leaned in to her, reached for her hands. "Evie, look at me. I didn't chase you down because we had sex, great or not. I came after you because I can't live without you, don't want to live without you. Because I need you." He paused, gearing for the words he needed her to hear; to believe. "Because I love you."

Turning fully to him allowed him to see the clouds in those normally clear blue eyes; the soul deep sadness—but, and his heart lifted just a fraction—maybe a hint of hope?

Groaning he leaned in further, resting his forehead against hers. "Oh darlin'," his voice a low whispered growl, "why did you leave without talking to me?"

She wasn't pulling punches. "You turned away from me."

He exhaled slowly, reliving the day before. The surprise, the confusion, the sorrow. Rethought his behavior. "I did, and I'm so sorry. But I figured without Mia in the picture..." he shrugged.

"Yes, without Mia in the picture. That was the crux, wasn't it? To be honest, I wasn't sure your offer would still stand."

"And I wasn't sure you'd want to stay." His thumb stroked the soft skin of her palm. "If you'd stayed we could have talked. We could have—" Her fingers closed over her palm, stilling him. Silencing him. Confused he broke contact, moved back slightly from her forehead, sought her eyes. And knew. For a moment he wasn't sure what he felt. Anger for all those gone by who'd hurt her? Sadness for the little girl others hadn't cared enough about?

Putting that to the side wasn't easy. Nor was this. "You thought I'd leave you." Frowning he moved on slowly, carefully. "Evie I can't undo your past, but if you love me, if you want a life with me, I promise that as long as it's in my power, I will not walk away. You can work wherever you want, we can live wherever you want—I just want us to be together and for you to be happy." He hitched one shoulder trying to lighten the tension. "It's true. It's in the Halligan genes. We come from a long line of boringly monogamous couples who are in it for the long haul."

Finally, he saw the light begin to change in her eyes. "Yeah? Personally, I've always found merit in boring."

That lightness was seeping into him. "Yeah? And?"

"This is what you really want?"

He nodded.

"Then, yes, I will." Her smile added the rest, but she offered words as well. "Judson Daniel Halligan, I will take boring—although that might change after we've filled that big house with all our own little hell-raisers." She laughed, to him a sound sweeter than any music, any birdcall. "I love you JD. And it scared me. Still does. But even more than loving you, I trust you. Trust you enough to walk beside you into the unknown, into all the unknowns that will face us in our future."

That was all he needed to hear. In one swoop he was on his feet, her in his arms, swinging her around like a crazy man. Hell, he *was* a crazy man. Crazy in love and she loved him back. "Darlin', I'll carry you through all those unknowns."

She shook her head. "No, you won't. You'll walk beside me, and we'll look after each other."

"Spoken like a true Halligan wife."

❧

SHE SCRAMBLED TO get down, and he eased her back, holding her until her feet, once more in those sky-high stilettos, touched the floor.

"I've kinda missed the shoes."

She emulated his one-eyebrow lift. "You have? Well, cowboy, I might have some other outfits in mind that could suit those shoes. But you'll have to wait until we get back home."

His responding grin stole her breath; lit him and he wasn't the only one. Evie felt like she was glowing. Knew she was glowing. JD loved her. And she loved him. It hadn't been about needing a mother for his niece, and she should have stayed to hear him out. Would now always hear him out.

The dream, the fairytale she never allowed herself to believe was for her, was coming true. If it was possible for her insides to be shooting fireworks, she knew that it would feel like this—like bubbles of heat shooting off in all directions.

One or two bubbles burst though when she noted his change of expression. Was he wondering what *home* meant? "JD? Did you mean it when you said we could work anywhere? Live anywhere?"

He nodded. "Yep. Absolutely, I really meant it. I just want to be with you."

"You'd give up the ranch?"

His eyes clouded. "Maybe not give up. But I was thinking Cody could run it, and we could come back for vacations."

Lord this was a man in a million. "Good, because I want to live—" She watched his face tighten, but couldn't tease him any longer. "At the ranch. With you."

His eyes narrowed, as though he didn't quite believe her. "Your work?"

"I resigned this morning." Her grin was impish, and she knew he'd work it out soon. "While I was sitting here."

"What?" His head swiveled, taking in their surroundings. "What about your flight?"

"Canceled that too. While I was sitting here. JD, when

you found me I was working up the courage to drive back. To tear strips off you, to warn you that if you ever locked me out again, there'd be consequences."

"Coming back?" He frowned, processing it all, letting it roll out. "Do you mean I went through all that—?"

She grinned again. "Consequences." In truth, she'd just needed him to say the words, been almost too terrified to speak; terrified he wouldn't say the ones she so badly needed to hear. To be sure *he* was sure.

Later she'd tell him all that. Thank him properly for not abandoning her. She'd also tell him of her plans to be a legal advocate for women in jeopardy, to help women like her mother—and like Cody's tenant, the woman she hadn't been able to completely get out of her mind, and who she suspected needed help.

Yes, all that would come later, for now though a little devil was at work inside her. "Besides, *most people* would have realized I was sitting at the wrong gate. This flight was heading out to Chicago. That's the San Francisco gate over there, the one you walked through. Flight left fifteen minutes ago."

His responding chuckle was slow at first then building. Deep, gravelly and sexy as hell, once more sliding over her nerve ends, bringing them to life, teasing her with delicious little fiery shoots that pinged around her body. *Did he really know what he did to her?*

"Is that right?" His mouth pulled in at the corners, cute,

sexy. "Okay, well, just maybe life isn't going to be as boring as I predicted. Though, I would have thought *most people* would be more considerate of the person they're going to marry."

She raised her arms, looping them around his neck, pulling his face to her. "Well, thank goodness neither of us are *most people*. Where would be the fun in that?"

"Amen to that darlin'."

Finally, his laughter echoed away and he did the thing she been longing for since he'd first found her. He kissed her. Whispered in her ear, and kissed her again.

And any lingering doubts fluttered away.

He really knew. He was sure—sure that *she* was what he wanted.

Just as she had never been more certain that her future was with JD Halligan.

That life, that future, stretched out before her—she and JD, the family they'd build. And all because of one tiny cherub. Who'd have guessed?

Maybe Mia did… The thought made her smile.

Maybe Mia would be a matchmaker…

THE END

Acknowledgements

I'm writing this at the end of March. March is a celebratory month for me this year as it marks the 30th anniversary of my first ever publishing contract. It was for a second-chance romance entitled *"No Replacements; No Guarantees"* and the publisher was Pan Macmillan. Just prior to that, I had been asked to join the first committee of the fledgling Romance Writers of Australia Association where I learned so much and made precious friendships that are strong to this day, friends in the trade, so to speak, who have supported me and whom I hope I have also supported as we've bumbled along, learning to survive in this unpredictable world of publishing.

My publishing contracts now number 84, and as I wrote this 81st book, I found myself being even more grateful to all those writer and publishing friends—some of them now passed, who played a role, and those who continue to play that role—in me reaching this stage of my career. To offer individual names would be like adding another novel, but if you're reading this, you know who you are—and I once more send my love and gratitude.

Of course, writer friends and publishers can only take

you so far. After that you need the most precious people of all—you, the reader. You are a vital part of our teams, the lifeblood of those teams. So, to you, goes my most humble and sincere gratitude.

Like raising a child, it takes a village to create a book, and for this particular book though, there are many people in that publishing sector I spoke of who need to be acknowledged. First of all, to my brilliant and patient editor, Kelly Hunter. (*By the way, it's customary to thank one's editor and publisher—manners, right? Sometimes though, those thanks are offered with even more depth and sincerity, and each time I thank my Tule team, or talk about them or even think about them, my gratitude is always at the deepest and most sincere level.*) So, Kelly—thank you for your support, your honesty, for your continued offers of a chat, for pushing me when it's needed and continuing to be on board with my characters and stories. For all that, I will always be grateful.

And the rest of the Tule team. Gosh—where to begin. Jane—you've been behind me since day one, and that kind of support and belief is absolutely priceless. It means more than you'll ever realize. Cyndi, Meghan, Lee and Mia—you've become more than just an editorial team, you've become friends and every email makes me smile. Thank you for all you do. And to lovely fellow Tule author, Nan Reinhardt, my first Tuligan friend—a warm, spunky and gracious lady on whom my own character Nan is based. *Surprise!*

One friend must be singled out and that's Paula J Beavan, historical writer extraordinaire who reads every manuscript, often several times, who comes up with brilliant ideas, lets me ramble and makes me laugh. Thank you. You too are priceless.

As always, I thank my beautiful family for their continued support and interest, most especially my wonderful husband who did all the cleaning and most of the cooking during the creation of this novel. And no, you cannot have him, he's mine.

Bless you all—I hope you enjoy JD and Evie's story.

MORE BOOKS BY KAZ DELANEY

Hart of Texas Murder Mysteries series

Book 1: *A Bittersweet Murder*

Book 2: *Preserving the Evidence*

Book 3: *Candy-Coated Conspiracy*

Book 4: *Murder Below the Mistletoe*

Book 5: *Cupid, Cupcakes and Carnage*

Book 6: *Dial M for Mud Cake*

Available now at your favorite online retailer!

ABOUT THE AUTHOR

Award winning YA & children's author, **Kaz Delaney**, and her alter ego, have currently sold 73 titles between them over a 26 year career.

Her books have won many awards, among them the prestigious **Aurealis Award** for best paranormal **and ARRA** (Australian Romance Readers Association) **awards.** Her novel '***Dead, Actually***' **(Allen & Unwin)** was nominated for a Davitt Award, (*Best crime novel, Sisters In Crime*) in the YA section. Dividing her time between teaching and writing, Kaz formerly tutored Creative Writing for CSU's Enrichment Program as well as teaching and creating courses for the Australian College of Journalism.

Having always had a love of cozy mysteries, Kaz is having so much fun writing her **Hart of Texas Murder Mystery Series** for **TULE Publishing**, that she worries it's not legal!

With their family grown and gone, Kaz lives with her wonderful husband at beautiful Lake Macquarie, Australia, a place she describes as a strip of land between the ocean and lake. Like Rosie, Kaz loves to bake and grow vegetables and unlike Rosie, manages to make a mess of every crochet task she undertakes.

Thank you for reading

The Cowboy's Baby Surprise

If you enjoyed this book, you can find more from all our great authors at TulePublishing.com, or from your favorite online retailer.

Printed in the USA
CPSIA information can be obtained
at www.ICGtesting.com
LVHW042152040924
790191LV00005B/93

9 781962 707763